Hidden

ISBN 9798374705737

Hidden

By

Barbara Barratt

Synopsis

Delia, Sue & Val have been firm friends since childhood. They grew up in the same village and after university – all of them going to different places and studying different things, they all end up back in their home village : Willington.

Sue is very involved in St. Aidan's church and drags her friends along to most things.....more willingly than she realises and generally gets involved with the happenings in the village, and occasionally does supply teaching in the local school.

Val loves her work as an event's organiser and is highly respected by her boss : Rodney Melker.

Delia is a high flying pharmacist with the mother in law from hell!

So how does the disappearance of Alice - the much loved Vicar's wife .....a shooting, and a head on car crash shake or strengthen their relationships?

Chapter 1

The gossip was rife. Sue & Val listened with rapt attention to the tale that Delia was imparting during their weekly coffee get togethers in their favourite coffee shop 'Mug's with Hugs'.

"So…. she who shall not be named", Sue interrupted .. "you need to stop reading so much Harry Potter – you and the 'she who shall not be named'"!

"So" resumed Delia, "Brenda heard the ruckus and saw her get in the car with a huge suitcase helped by Dennis the demon Archdeacon. She couldn't miss it really as she was cycling up the lane past the vicarage to get into church to sort the flowers. Poor Brenda, she was so shocked she fell backwards over the hedge!"

With that they all laughed and Val nearly choked on the cookie she was devouring.

"What you mean is, she was so busy nosying at what was going on that she fell off her bike. But lets face it" said Sue, "if anyone knows what's going on, Brenda will know – or think she knows! Seriously though Delia, are you sure that Alice had a suitcase with her? What on earth would she be doing going off with Dreadful Dennis, he's absolutely notorious for flirting with any woman under 90, and if what you are saying holds water, it looks like she's moved in with him".

"Well that's just it" said Delia, "neither of them have been seen since and apparently the powers that be up at 'Church Mansion' are getting concerned".

"It's Brian that I feel sorry for", piped up Val, who had been listening carefully since completing the weekly ecstasy ritual of a double chocolate chip cookie which she'd nearly choked on a few moments ago, "you couldn't meet a nicer fella – even if he is a vicar" she said as an after thought. “He always seemed so lonely until he met Alice, and despite the age difference they seemed genuinely happy. She was good for him. He seemed so much more relaxed with everyone and even his sermons improved ”, laughed Val.

The three of them pondered this in silence whilst they drank their coffee.

“Just going off the subject.... have either of you heard any more about the shooting in town last week – I’ve heard a rumour that they’ve made an arrest” said Sue.

“No, nothing definite” replied Val, “but I really hope they get the person — the family must be devastated”.

Sue, Val & Delia had been friends since childhood. They had gone through primary school and secondary school together and even when they went off to university all over the country, they kept in touch meeting most months at one of the colleges.

Sue finished her teaching qualification and came home and married her childhood sweet heart Neil. They married in the village church: St. Aidan’s, Willington - the topic of their present conversation, with Val and Delia as bridesmaids. That was over fifteen years ago. Neil ran a very successful plumbing business in the area and when Sue had her first child, she gave up teaching at a neighbouring school to become a full time mum, help with Neil’s business, run the brownie pack and generally enjoy village life. Since then Sue had gone on to have another two children both of who were in school. Her youngest Bobby had started reception in September. Her oldest boy Adam was in year 6 and would be going to the local high school at the end of this school year. Sue’s second child – Flora was in year 4. Sue loved being a mum and also loved her involvement in the church and the village and only missed teaching when it came to Christmas, as she always organised the nativity, but she didn't miss it when it came to report writing! Sue occasionally did the odd day supply teaching at the village school and was happy to help with the PTA. So to hear that Alice had left Brian, upset the balance of village life as she knew it.

Since the by-pass had been built Willington was off the beaten track. You wouldn't really go looking for it, and you wouldn't just come across it. So the only time there was more than the villagers was when there was a village fair that was widely advertised. The people of Willington were, on the whole a lovely bunch which made it a really pleasant village to live in, where everyone got on with their own lives but would be there if you needed them……. until the day that Alice, the vicars wife went off with Dennis the Dreadful!

Brian was 10 years older than Alice. Their accidental meeting five years earlier happened after Brian had been at Willchester Cathedral a few weeks before Christmas.

The temperature had dropped considerably during the afternoon and when he came onto the street, the flags glistened with the frost. He thought about doing some Christmas shopping - he considered going to get the perfume for his sister whilst he had some spare time. He briskly made his way down the narrow street towards the car park. The town was clearly busy with shoppers and visitors to the Christmas market that had gone up a few days before.

He realised a little too late that he turned the corner rather fast only to collide with a young lady struggling with parcels and trying to stay upright in her high heels on the frosty ground. Down she went, along with her parcels and Brian on top! That day he fell, quite literally 'head over heals' and when their eyes met he knew that he'd found the love he had been waiting for. The lady in question was, of course - Alice.

Slipping and sliding on the icy pavement Brian got himself up and apologised repeatedly as he helped Alice who was somewhat shaken by the collision. Once she had regained her composure and retrieved all her parcels, she took stock of the man who had charged into her with what seemed like the ferocity of a pit bull and looked up into the kind and concerned face of a very handsome chap. When Brian offered to take her for a drink, by way of an apology, she hesitated only for a moment. She could do with a sit down after her argument with the pavement and a warm drink would certainly help dispel the cold that was starting to seep through her body.

Brian took her parcels from her and led her by the arm to the tea rooms not far from the Cathedral. It was warm and cosy inside with pretty tablecloths and the inviting smell of freshly brewed coffee.

"Hello Brian" shouted Molly from the counter, "we've not seen you for while – are you OK"?

"Hello Molly, yes I'm fine thanks" responded Brian. It was the place he visited when he came into Willchester. The food was all home made and Molly's mum made the most delicious home made cakes.

Brian handed the menu to Alice as she said "do you come in here often"? At which they looked at each other and laughed! Brian explained that when he came into Willchester he always called in for something to eat.

"Now… I don't know your name" as he gazed into Alice's beautiful green eyes feeling that he could be swallowed whole as he sank into her stare, then realised that she had just spoken to him!

"I'm sorry – what did you say" asked Brian……. "I said" repeated Alice "that I don't know your name either" and laughed at his expression.

"Silly me" said Brian, "I'm Brian" he said as he held out his hand…….. "and I'm Alice" said this engaging young woman with whom he was becoming more and more besotted by the minute.

As he held her delicate hand Molly came over and asked what she could get them.

"What do you recommend, Brian" asked Alice "you come in here a lot, so what would you suggest?"

"Well", said Brian, "I think after the jolt you've just had a luxury hot chocolate would be in order, and Molly, whatever the cake of the day is, would be delightful, please."

"Right you are " said Molly, "coming up"!

Alice started to undo her coat, and took her scarf and gloves off as Brian exclaimed how warm it was in the tea rooms.

As Brian took his coat off he observed the strangest look on Alice's face : of course, he had his 'dog collar' on which wasn't visible when his coat was fastened up – but it was a look he had seen many times before!

"Ah" said Brian and touched the collar, as Alice looked into his face. "Is this a problem for you?"

For a moment Alice said nothing, she looked at Brian. Then she said "No, it's not a problem at all. But I'm not very religious! What are you – Catholic?"

Brian laughed and said "No, I'm an Anglican Vicar – Church of England".

"Oh, that's OK then" said Alice. "My Mum's Church of England and I suppose I am really, not that I go to church very often, but if I was asked I would say that I was C of E – you know, like they ask you in hospital"...... she had started to garble a little and stopped abruptly as she saw that Brian was trying to contain a small smile from breaking out into a huge grin.

Just then, Molly brought their drinks and cakes. The steaming hot chocolate looked and smelled delicious as it was topped with fresh cream and marshmallows, and the cake – today's special of lemon & cinnamon looked equally divine.

The conversation stopped as both Alice and Brian lifted their drinks. For a few moments neither of them spoke while they enjoyed the creamy hot chocolate and heavenly light cake.

Almost at the same time Alice and Brian started to speak. "Oh dear" said Brian, "shall we try that again? After you Alice, what were you asking?"

"No, no, after you please, what were you about to say"? Said Alice a little shyly.

"Well" started Brian, "I was about to ask you where you were rushing to when I brought you down with an almighty collision……. along with, where do you work……. what do you do with your time and would you like to have dinner with me"? That all came out very quickly, but Brian knew that if he didn't ask this beautiful woman out he may never see her again, and he so wanted to see her again!

Alice laughed with great abandon and when she stopped said "Brian, the look on your face is priceless. Haven't you ever asked a girl out before?"

"Well, to be honest Alice" said Brian, "it's rather a long time since I did, and I'm rather out of practise!"

"Yes, I thought so" replied Alice who then took a long drink from her hot chocolate and ate a piece of cake while she considered the invitation she had just received. Brian was certainly very handsome and she was really enjoying his company now that she had thawed out, but he was a Vicar! As she looked at Brian he started to say "I'm sorry, I'm sorry, I really shouldn't have asked, a lovely girl like you must have a string of young men just waiting to take you out….."

Alice looked straight at him and said "I would be delighted to have dinner with you , and no, I do not have either a string of young men, or any young man wanting to take me out - except you, it would seem."

"Oh, that's wonderful Alice! Would Saturday evening suit, though I do have to get up early on Sunday – that's my busy day"! Commented Brian as they both laughed.

"Saturday would be wonderful" said Alice. "Now finish your drink before it goes cold and if you don't eat that delicious cake – I might just eat it for you " said Alice, now very comfortable with this charming man.

That was five years ago and plenty of dinners, lunches and outings took place following that afternoon before Brian proposed to Alice six months after their first meeting.

The congregation at St. Aidan's had noticed a definite change in their Vicar during those six months. Whilst Brian was always kind and devoted to his congregation, they noticed a lightness in him…. He was less serious and more inclined to make a joke, as well as take a joke, than he had been in the four years he had been with them. Most of the more 'mature' ladies in the congregation had suggested that there must be a female on his arm, so when this beautiful auburn haired beauty arrived at morning service at the beginning of the school holidays wearing an exquisite diamond ring, and was later introduced by Brian to members of the congregation over coffee, as "my fiancé", no one was very surprised. Most were absolutely delighted and offered to help plan the wedding! One or two of the younger women were decidedly disappointed as they rather hoped they had a chance with Brian themselves!

Chapter 2

Alice and Brian were married at St. Aidan's on a beautiful warm sunny day the following June with the Bishop of Willchester officiating. The church was full to bursting with their friends, family and the many parishioners who had taken both Brian and Alice to their hearts. The choir learned some new music (which was almost unheard of) and even recruited a few more volunteers for the occasion and sang as they had never sung before. Some of the regular parishioners were heard to say later that they even sang in tune for the first time!

The reception was held at the big old Parish Hall which the parishioners had decked out with flowers, bunting and ribbons. The catering was done by Gerry at the local deli who told Brian that no expense would be spared as Brian turned slightly green at the suggested overall cost for the catering and when he tried to get the deli to compromise was told that only the best would do for him and Alice. Whilst Brian thought that he would give Alice anything, his stipend wasn't quite in the Rothschild bracket and he had several sleepless nights worrying about the catering for the reception. Little did Brian know that Freddie Fishington (better known to the congregation as 'Farting Freddie') had told Gerry at the deli to send him the bill for the catering. Freddie had attended St. Aidan's all his life and seen many a vicar come and go. After the problems they had encountered with some of the clergy over the years Brian was a joy to work with. He never complained, welcomed everyone, was delighted when people offered help and always got stuck in himself .

Freddie was a self made man. He'd made shed loads of money through good enterprise and deals on the stock market and was a most generous benefactor of St. Aidan's. He was a large, well fed man with a loud jovial laugh – when you heard it you knew that Freddie was about. He was only too delighted to pick up the tab for Brian & Alice's wedding, which he told Brian a few days later when he saw Brian walking towards the library looking very peeky.

"Morning Brian", said Freddie "and how are the wedding plans coming along"?

"Hello Freddie" replied Brian. "Well everything's more or less organised…."

"I hear a but coming along" said Freddie…… "is there a problem?"

After considerable hesitation Brian explained to Freddie that he couldn't seem to make Gerry understand that they had a strict budget for the wedding reception, particularly as Alice's parents weren't able to contribute a great deal.

"Oh is that all" said Freddie, to an increasingly perplexed looking Brian.

"Freddie, 'is that all' is a considerable worry to me. I want it to be lovely, but all the things that Gerry wants to do are just beyond my means, and he won't take no for answer!"

"Oh Brian, Brian, Brian….." said Freddie laughing gently, "I'm so sorry, I really should have told you before. You will **not** be paying for the reception – it's all taken care of and I've given Gerry instructions for 'no expense spared'."

"Freddie, what on earth do you mean – it's all been taken care of?" asked Brian.

"Brian, it's all taken care of. Gerry will send the bill to me", and as Brian opened his mouth to speak Freddie continued "there's no argument about this. It is my greatest pleasure and honour to do this for you. When I needed a friend the most, you were with me. You sat with Grace, Tom and me when Pat was dying. You helped Grace & Tom come to terms with the loss of their mother and have always been there for me since.

There have been plenty of vicar's at St. Aidan's in my time, and plenty we've been glad to see the back of I might add! That's not the case with you. You're highly regarded, respected and loved by so many people....... and your wedding is the talk of the village – everyone wants to make it special".

"Freddie, I really can't let you do this" said Brian.

"Tish Tosh" said Freddie, "It's done.... It's a wedding present and let's face it Brian, I can afford it" said Freddie laughing his infectious laugh so loudly that Brian was compelled to join in.

"Now be gracious Brian.... Just accept defeat and we'll all have a jolly good time".

Knowing that Freddie was not going to take no for an answer he simply said, "Well Freddie, thank you" and warmly shook the older man by his hand, knowing that he must concede defeat and also knowing that a great weight had been lifted from his shoulders.

Chapter 3

The wedding of Brian and Alice was a glorious day for everyone. The sun shone, Alice was a stunning bride in a white shimmering dress and veil with the most perfect

bouquet of pale pink roses to match her bridesmaids dresses. No one could have been happier. Brian beamed at everyone and pure joy shone from him.

Brian had asked Freddie to be his best man and Freddie glowed with pride when he gave the rings to be blessed. A very special friendship had developed between Brian and Freddie, despite Freddie being considerably older and Brian being very different. In Freddie's eyes, Brian was almost like another son or younger brother and he felt

honoured to be Brian's best man on this glorious June day.

The Parish Hall saw considerable merry making that evening. The speeches alone had the guests in uproar. Particularly the bride's father who repeatedly said that he got the shock of his life when Alice said she was going to marry a Vicar! He said that he kept asking her if she was sure he was a vicar and not just going to a fancy dress party, but then added that if he had been, he should have gone as a Bishop as he wore his favourite football team colours!

Everyone took this in good humour and would talk about the speeches for a long time to come, especially Brian when he spoke of his great love for Alice and his hopes for the future. There was not a dry eye to be seen.

Sue recalled that all this was nearly five years ago and lots of good things had been achieved at St. Aidan's in that time.

"Anyway", said Sue, "will I see you two renegades in church on Sunday. I'm after helpers for the Easter Eggstravaganza, and I could do with you two to help me round up a few people on Sunday".

"Yeah, Ok then" said Val and Delia joined in by saying "hmm, it might be quite interesting on Sunday considering…... I'll be there".

"What do you mean Delia?" asked Val.

"Well with what we've heard about Alice, I expect a lot of people will want to know what's happened and I expect Brenda will have told everyone by then".

"Oh dear" replied Sue "I didn't think of that. Poor Brian. There must be something we can do".

"Yes, there probably is" , suggested Val, "and one of the best ways would be to recruit people to help with the Easter Eggstravaganza event instead of them talking about

Alice. So, yes. I'll definitely be there. I know I'm not as regular an attendee as you Sue, but Brian doesn't deserve this, so we should help however we can. I really can't imagine what that silly girl is thinking of……… Dennis the dreadful indeed!"

Thanks, you two" said Sue, who since becoming Church Warden was feeling a little bit protective of Brian, and made a mental note to phone him later. "If I don't see you before I'll see you on Sunday morning."

With that the three friends parted company with Sue wondering if this story was as true as Delia had made out, and if so, just how she and Neil could support Brian. Sue was going to pick up some meat from the village butcher for their evening meal on her way home. As she walked towards the butcher's she saw Brian on the other side of the road. His head was down and he definitely looked lost in thought, miles away in fact. She thought about attracting his attention but decided to leave him to his own thoughts for the time being.

There were a number of people in the butcher's and a lot of conversation taking place, but as she entered she noticed Brenda in the queue doing most of the talking. As

Sue quietly waited her turn she could clearly hear Brenda ……

"Well I've known for some time that things weren't right in that vicarage…… she wouldn't join in with anything and poor Brian was having to get his own meals as she never seemed to be here. It's not right I tell you… a Vicar's wife should be at the hub of the village….." and then Brenda stopped abruptly as she noticed Sue looking at her stony faced.

Tony the butcher had noticed Sue come in and that she was listening to Brenda. He hadn't got a lot of time for Brenda really, she was the village gossip, but if what she was claiming to have seen was true then it was a damn shame for Brian.

"Now then Brenda", said Tony firmly "I think you should just let it go….. Alice may just have gone on holiday for a while and you might be doing her a dis-service."

"I know what I saw" announced an indignant Brenda….. And before she could say another word Sue said " Yes, Brenda, and that's the trouble with you – you see things without your glasses on and get it wrong … look at the time you told everyone that Denise was pregnant because she'd been a bit sick in church one morning…..hmm, yes…. remember that one do you?".

"Yes, well, I didn't know she'd been out at a party the night before and had one glass of wine too many……" stuttered Brenda.

"No, and that's the problem" said Sue "you don't know what you see – you make up most of it. I remember that one only too well. You could have caused a divorce between Denise and Dave a few months ago, making such a suggestion."

Unknown to Brenda, Dave had had the 'snip' after their third child was born.

Thankfully Dave had been at the party with Denise…. It had been at Sue's house to celebrate Neil's 40th birthday but Sue wasn't going to give Brenda the satisfaction of telling her that.

"Now I suggest that you refrain from any more comments about Brian and Alice before you do more damage" said Sue....

"Yes, but I know….." started Brenda….

"ENOUGH", said Sue in a very loud voice. "Leave it be Brenda" continued Sue, "before people start talking about you and that man from the A…..."

"OK, OK" said Brenda making a hasty retreat….. "I've got things to do…. I'll get my meat tomorrow" and Brenda left the butchers at great speed.

Tony finished serving the customers in front of Sue. The shop was empty now, apart from Sue. As he turned to serve Sue he said "I just can't believe that Alice has just gone off like that. She used to come in here full of the joys of spring and seemed really happy here in the village and with Brian".

Sue nodded and added" She is a little shy, but she was starting to come out of herself. Of course it's difficult when you have a full time job, and be a Vicar's wife, but she was always lovely and friendly with people."

"I must say though Sue" added Tony, "she hasn't seemed herself the last few times I've seen her. She hasn't looked very well and seemed to be distracted. I just hope all these rumours aren't true. It would be such a shame – especially for Brian……he seemed overjoyed when they got married."

"I couldn't agree more" replied Sue, "that's why I think its all a bit strange".

"Well if there is anything I can do " said Tony, "just let me know….. I like Brian, always have, and he was wonderful with my Mum when she was poorly…." "OK Tony, if I think of anything I'll let you know" said Sue as Tony finished putting her meat in a bag.

As she looked at the time Sue realised that she had been out a little longer than she had anticipated. She had planned to get the evening meal started before she collected the children from school but she was running a bit later than planned.

She needed to have a talk with Neil when the children were out of ear shot….. They were just getting to the age where they listened to conversations but got the gist of them wrong!

Chapter 4

Val hadn't been feeling too well for a few days but had met Sue & Delia as planned for their weekly get together. Val usually had Thursday off but did some work from home. Since leaving university with a degree in Business Studies, she had done a variety of jobs but ten years ago had found herself running the 'Events for All' Company after Rodney Melker, to whom she was PA, had had a heart attack. Thankfully he had survived, but it had made him re-assess his working life. His company was very successful and he could afford to let someone else run it so that he could enjoy time with his much loved wife and children. It was a profitable company and he knew that Val knew as much about organising events as he did and she had a great way with the clients as well as the staff. Val was very career minded and showed no inclination to wanting a family. Val's husband, Rupert, was frequently abroad with his high powered job in computer technology so Rodney decided to make Val his CEO. Val had blossomed and loved the work.

Val's beautiful four bedroom detached house on the edge of the village was the envy of many people, but thankfully that did not include her oldest friends Sue & Delia. Mary, the cleaner had just left so Val knew as she entered the hall that her house would be immaculate.

As she entered the hall Val went light headed and thought that she might faint. She quickly got hold of the banister to steady herself and decided to have a lie down.

Carefully Val went upstairs to the bedroom that had recently been re-decorated in beautiful pale greens and cream and kicking off her shoes climbed under the duvet. As she closed her eyes she reflected on the conversation with Sue and Delia.

She thought back to the beautiful wedding of Brian and Alice and the love that was so obvious between them. Whilst she wasn't a regular church goer, Val did go on special occasions and was always willing to help Sue with the events that she organised. Brian and Alice were always there, helping and chatting with people. Brian had even agreed to have wet sponges thrown at him the summer before as part of the church fete and Alice gladly paid her money to join in. Val was smiling when she recalled the laughter between them as she fell asleep.

Val was still asleep when Rupert gently woke her up with a kiss…… "what's all this, sleeping in the afternoon?" asked Rupert as a drowsy Val came round.

"Oh, hello darling, I didn't expect you back until later this evening" responded Val.

"I managed to get an earlier flight, and I thought I would get home to you and we would go out for a lovely meal" replied Rupert.

Val visibly paled at the thought of food. Rupert was concerned as Val loved to eat out and could see that she had no enthusiasm for a meal out tonight.

"When did you start feeling unwell, Val"? asked Rupert. "Well I've not been feeling quite right for a week or so, but I thought I'd just picked up a bug, or something" replied Val. "I'm sorry, Rupes, but I don't think I could face a meal out tonight, do you mind"?

Rupert knew that Val was obviously 'under the weather' as this was so out of character, she was always fighting fit and full of life.

"No, my lovely, I don't mind at all. You stay there and I'll go and make some drinks and we'll have a quiet night in" said Rupert just wanting to take care of his beautiful wife.

While Rupert was making drinks for himself and Val he thought about the day he had met her some six years before. The company he worked for did all sorts of computer analysing and setting up systems and he had been with the company since he left school. The directors were looking for a merger and had employed the Events for All Company to do a huge marketing event. Rupert would turn his hand to anything if asked and on the occasion of the marketing event had rolled his sleeves up to stabilise a gazebo that wasn't very secure and was in danger of being taken away with the wind. With his sleeves rolled up, tie undone, jacket slung over a chair and perspiration dripping down his face, he looked up to see this tall dark haired beauty glaring down at him.

"What on earth do you think you are doing" said Val.

"Well I'm trying to make sure that this gazebo doesn't blow away and cause any damage as the company that put it up haven't done a very good job" exclaimed Rupert.

"Now just wait a minute….. My workers had it all in hand until you came along as superman to take over" retorted Val.

"They didn't look as if they had anything in hand" replied Rupert, "or I wouldn't have had to roll my sleeves up"!

The exchange between the two of them was becoming heated and Rupert smiled at the memory of it.

Before any more words, heated or otherwise could be exchanged Rodney came over and said to Val, "Ah, I see you've met Rupert" he said to Val. "He's going far… he'll be running this company before long! Hello Rupert, how are you" said Rodney shaking his hand. " I can see that you've acquainted yourself with my right hand man - well woman" laughed Rodney. "Val is the power behind the throne - she knows all there is to know of my company, and I rely on her

totally".

With that Rupert bowed gracefully to Val whose annoyance dissolved at this jesture!

“It’s lovely to see you Rodney” said Rupert “you’re looking well…. How are you coping without all the stress of work” he added with a smile.

“I’m well, thanks Rupert, but that heart attack brought me to my senses. You can work and work until you drop…. then what ….. You end up fit for nothing and everyone loses out. I’m lucky that I’ve got Val here…...she’s an absolute marvel….I don’t know what I would have done without her…..” He smiled gently and touched her arm. Rodney was very fond of Val along with Rodney’s wife Chrissy, who knew that the trust Rodney had in her had helped him recover from his heart attack. Rupert noticed the fond gesture from Rodney and was quite touched as Val tried to pooh pooh it away, saying that she was just doing her job. Rupert, however, could see that it was much more than that........ She clearly cared about Rodney.

The event that Val had organised went like a dream. The gazebo that Rupert had secured, stayed secure much to Val’s amusement! By the time the day ended Val had been on her feet for some ten hours or more, but despite the exhaustion that she felt she still looked poised and elegant and was happily talking to all the guests.

Rupert had been observing her on and off all day and was really desperate to get to know her.

As the team started to clear away he went over to Val and asked her if she would like him to unsecure the gazebo! With that she laughed out loud and saw the twinkle in Rupert’s eye as he was clearly teasing her. Val could see that he was actually quite attractive and agreed to give him her phone number though she wasn’t really sure that she was his ‘type'.

He was definitely a high flyer and from what she had overheard from people during the day, Rupert was destined for great things in the company. Anyway............. She wouldn’t hold her breath to see if he phoned!

The following day – Sunday, Val was having a well earned lie in . Her one bedroom flat was her pride and joy as she had worked so hard to buy it. Her Mum & Dad had wanted to help her but she insisted on saving for it herself as they had seen her through university and she had a younger sister now studying who needed their help. It had taken her a while and she had lived at home until she had the deposit.

The flat was just on the edge of the village and was part of a newly built block. It was fairly exclusive as it was near some park land that boasted a few pretty walks and the flats tended to be owned by yuppies! This always made Val laugh as she didn't consider herself to be one.

Just as she was thinking about taking a leisurely bath with lots of bubbles, her phone rang. She didn't recognise the number so hesitated in answering in case it was work as she really needed to have a break from work today. Reluctantly she decided to answer the call.

"Well good morning, Miss. Walker" came a voice that sounded familiar but she couldn't place for a moment.

"Good morning.... Who is this?" Val asked somewhat hesitantly.

"You haven't forgotten the gazebo builder already" said Rupert, sounding very upbeat and lively.

"Aahhh..... Of course.... I thought the voice was familiar" said Val. "How are you this morning Mr. Gazebo builder?" She said smiling. "You're up and about early for a Sunday, especially after the hectic event yesterday".

"Early Miss. Walker..... It's after 11..... Don't say that you're not up and about!" Val could hear the smile on his face as he said it.

"Well I did have a very busy day yesterday..... In fact I had a very busy couple of weeks to get yesterday sorted and ready" Val replied slightly indignant but laughing a little too.

“So... how soon can you be ready?” asked Rupert.

“Ready for what?” asked Val.

“Well I thought I would take you out for lunch as it’s such a lovely day... And you did work very hard yesterday supervising all those gazebo builders” laughed Rupert.

Val laughed in spite of herself but was a little bit lost for words. She had felt a very unfamiliar tingle down her back as she listened to Rupert’s silky voice. She wasn’t sure what to do as she had planned a lazy day at home catching up on the usual domestic things that get left when you’re working full time, and particularly after the last two weeks of manic preparations .

“Val, Val, are you still there.......” she heard the voice at the other end of the phone asking...“Oh yes...sorry Rupert, I was just thinking... I’ve got such a lot of catching up to do ....”. “You can catch up some other time” came the silky voice , “I really want to see you again....please say you’ll come for lunch” pleaded Rupert.

Val laughed and hesitantly said “OK then, but I’m not nearly ready”.

“That’s fine...shall we say an hour? I’ll pick you up”.

“OK I can be ready in about an hour” promised Val and gave Rupert her address.

Chapter 5

Val put down the phone and realised that she hadn't asked Rupert where they were going. Whilst she ran the bath she went to her wardrobe. Val had a considerable wardrobe of good quality clothes, but they were mostly clothes for work.

As it was such a lovely day she chose a pair of light cotton trousers with a top and jacket. As she lowered herself into the bath she started to wonder why she had agreed to go out when she was really rather tired from the last two weeks of planning and had all sorts of jobs to do!

She closed her eyes and soaked into the bubbles for a little while thinking about Rupert and the gazebo the day before and as it brought a smile to her face she knew why she had agreed to go out with him.

Rupert was rather a charmer but she could tell that he had a sense of humour which Val thought was a necessary quality in any relationship.....

Forty five minute later, just as she was putting the finishing touches to her make- up, Val's door bell rang. As she opened it she was greeted with an enormous bunch of beautiful flowers and Rupert peering from behind. Val was a little stunned for a moment as she hadn't had anyone buy her such beautiful flowers for a long time.............

"Well aren't you going to ask me in? " enquired Rupert.

"Oh yes, of course......I was just a little taken aback by the flowers – I've not had anyone bring me flowers for a long time" responded Val. "Come on in, I am just about ready but I wasn't entirely sure what to wear as you didn't tell me where we are going".

As Rupert followed her into the flat she noticed that he was looking very dapper in lovely casual trousers, and open necked, short sleeved shirt.

“Well, we’ll just have to remedy that” said Rupert.....

“Remedy what?” replied Val....

“Flowers...... Someone bringing you flowers” said Rupert with a twinkle in his eye! “You look absolutely fine.... Well no, not fine...... you look gorgeous” said Rupert as he smiled a smile that not only made Val blush slightly, but made her tingle all over!She was also lost for words which was something not often said about Val!

They stood for a moment with Val not quite sure what to say. Swiftly she picked up the flowers and put them in the sink with water.

“I’ll put them in a vase when we get back” said Val, breaking the silence between them.

“OK then “ said Rupert, “If you have everything you need, we’ll get moving”.

“I’ll just get my bag and jacket” said Val “and I’ll be with you”.

Val went into her bedroom, slipped on her shoes, picked up her bag and jacket and had one last look in the mirror to check that her make up was ok and wondered what today would bring never thinking that today would really be the ‘first day of the rest of her life’!

Chapter 6

When Sue got home from the Thursday girls meeting in 'Mugs with Hugs' and the revelations about Alice going round in her head, she wanted to talk to Neil to see what he thought they should do but he had been called out to an emergency repair and didn't know what time he would be back. She would also need to go and collect the children from school in a little while so she didn't have much time to think. Making herself a cup of tea she started to think about the situation.

She got on well with Brian but had only been the Church Warden for a short time and didn't want to seem nosy, but she did want to help in whatever way she could. Sue had always got on with Alice who she found very easy to talk to once she had settled in.

Alice worked as an examinations officer for one of the exam boards that had a big office in town. That was how Brian had met her. She remembered Alice telling her the tale of how she slipped when Brian turned the corner quickly. Sue couldn't believe that Alice had just gone off like that, particularly with Dreadful Dennis! She did think that Alice had looked a bit strained the last couple of times she had seen her, but nothing to indicate that she might be leaving.

After some contemplation about what to do, she decided to email Brian. She explained that she had heard a 'rumour' about Alice leaving and asked if he was ok and whether there was anything either she or Neil could do to help. Having sent the email she thought that Brian would get in touch with her when he was ready.

When she looked at the time she knew she had better get moving to collect the children. Just as she was about to leave, the phone rang. Sue hesitated for a moment as she didn't want to be late but picked up the phone.

“Oh thank goodness I’ve got you” said Delia at the other end.

“What’s the matter Delia, you sound a bit panicked” said Sue recognising her friends voice immediately.

“Can you collect the children from school for me.... Jack’s been in an accident and I need to get to the hospital” said Delia.

“Oh my goodness” replied Sue “Is he Ok? What’s happened”.

“I’m not sure” said Delia, “I’ve just got this garbled message from the hospital. Please don’t tell the children though. I’ll ring you as soon as I know something”.

“Ok. I’ll bring the children here and feed them and say that you’ve been called out. You go, and Delia, please ring me when you know something” said Sue.

“ Thanks Sue, I don’t know what I’d do without you” replied Delia.

“Go on with you.... and Delia”said Sue ”Drive carefully”.

With that they hung up and Sue hurried off to collect the children from school.

Delia’s two children and Sue’s youngest two were in the same classes. Sue & Delia were pregnant at the same time but weeks apart. Sue’s oldest son Adam would be going into Year 7 in September and she was already getting nervous about him going to High School and which one to send him to. Delia’s oldest Maisie was 8 and in the same class as Flora, Sue’s daughter who would celebrate her eighth birthday in June. Robert (Bobby as they called him) was 6 and best friends with Joe – Delia’s youngest and he would be 6 in May.

On the whole, the children got on really well together. Adam, being the oldest, tended to be a bit bossy at times, but he had his own friends and was ‘growing up’ fast.

Both Sue & Delia felt quite blessed that the children they had were in the same classes and that they were 'besties' as the girls liked to say! That wasn't to say that they didn't fall out from time to time – but it usually only took a couple of days for them to make up.

Sue got to the school gates just as classes were being dismissed. Bobby was skipping out of class with Joe at his side. Bobby saw his Mum and ran to her as Joe came up behind. Before Joe could ask Sue said ,

"Your Mum's got delayed on a call out Joe, so you and Maisie are coming back with me for tea. Is that OK?"

Bobby said "Oh great. We can play that new game on the computer", before Joe even had time to respond.

"Is that ok?" asked Sue again, looking at Joe.

"Yes" he said a little hesitantly.

"Is something the matter Joe" asked Sue...... "you can tell me" she said laughing.

"Well....... It's just that Mum said we could have pizza tonight, it's my favourite" said Joe a bit shyly.

"Oh well, that's no problem at all" said Sue just as Flora and Maisie got to the gate.

"Hello love" Sue addressed Flora.

"What's not a problem, Mum?" asked Flora having overheard the end of the

conversation.

"We're having pizza tonight. Auntie Delia has got delayed so Joe and Maisie are

coming back with us for tea. Is that ok Maisie?" asked Sue.

"Thanks auntie Sue. I know that Joe was looking forward to pizza tonight – it's his favourite " she said in a conspiratorial way.

Sue winked at her and said "OK you guys, we need to get going. Where's Adam?" she asked Flora, just as he came strolling across the playground with one of his friends.

"Mum, Mum" he shouted as he got a bit closer, "can I go to Steven's for a bit so that we can do some of our project together".....

"And what project is this" asked Sue as Steven got a bit closer.

"It's a new one we've started today, Mrs. Newton" said Steven to Sue. "It's all about space travel and we've got a telescope at home".

Sue wanted to check that it was alright for Adam to go with Steven, but couldn't see Steven's Mum, Joyce. Just as she was considering this request, she heard a voice behind her shouting :

"Sue, I'm here" . It was Joyce almost running and looking a little fraught.

"Are you alright Joyce" asked Sue. Suc had known Joyce for years and she was a stalwart on the PCC even if she was a little dizzy!

Yes. I'm fine but I got delayed at the dentist. We had a patient who didn't like needles and almost fainted on us ." Joyce worked part time as a dental nurse at a nearby surgery. She had an older child Laura, at high school but wanted to be able to pick Steven up from school until he got into year 6.

"Mum" said Steven to Joyce. "Please can Adam come home with us so that we can use dad's telescope? We've just started a new project on space today".

Joyce looked at Sue and said "It's ok with me, if it's ok with you".

"If you like" said Joyce, "Adam can stay for tea and I'll drop him off later as I need to pick Laura up from school. She's got a rehearsal for the play at school."

“If you are sure, Joyce, and Adam is ok with that?” asked Sue as both Adam and Steven nodded their heads furiously.

“Well I think that’s settled” said Joyce. “We’ll see you later”. As Joyce, Steven and Adam went in one direction Joe took one hand and Bobby took the other and Sue walked the children back to their house with Flora and Maisie walking behind giggling away about something.

Chapter 7

The heating had just come on when Sue and the children got in the house. For early March the weather was pleasant but cool.

Sue sent the children to play once they had shed their coats and bags but did remind them that if they had homework to do they should do it before they had tea. A few mumbles from the girls meant that they did have something but Bobby and Joe just had their reading books tonight and Sue decided to sit with them later and they could read to her in turn.

Sue looked at the phone in case there was a message from Delia but as there was no flashing light there was no waiting message. It had only been about an hour since Delia's phone call so she may not have been at the hospital for long.

Sue went to bring in the washing that she had put outside earlier and started to think about Delia. Delia was probably the most clever of the three friends. She was very modest about her first class honours degree in science, and her pharmaceutical experience.

The three girls had made friends at primary school and stayed friends ever since. This in itself was quite remarkable really particularly as they had all moved away from home when they went to university. They had stayed in touch however, even when Delia had met her husband Jack in her first year at university when Jack was in the third year.

Sue and Val knew that Delia was besotted when they got together for a weekend after Delia had told them about Jack. After meeting Jack a couple of times Sue and Delia understood why Delia was so besotted. He had a really great sense of fun but was absolutely passionate about research into new drugs, and he was tall, blonde and very pleasant on the eyes! Jack came from the North East and when he finished University got a research job not far from his parent's home. His father was not in good health and he wanted to be near to help, as his sister had two small children.

When Delia finished with such a good degree, she had no problem having a choice of jobs and it was no surprise to her friends that she took the one nearest to where Jack was.

It wasn't always easy for Delia when she moved to be near Jack as his mother was somewhat protective of her relationship with her son, and thought that Delia was stealing him away.

Sue recalled a weekend the three friends shared to discuss bridesmaids dresses following her engagement to Neil on Graduation Day, when Delia shared with them how possessive of her son Jack's mother was. She told them that she didn't think there was a future for them together as his mother was constantly demanding him to do things for her even when she knew they had plans. So Delia told them that she had started looking for a job nearer home and by pure fluke had seen a job advertised in Willington at one of the big chemists. She had contacted them before the weekend and been offered an interview the following Monday so she had taken a couple of days off before she went back to the North East.

Delia told them that she hadn't told Jack that she was staying longer for an

interview, she thought it best to wait and see what happened first, but it did mean that they could have another night together!

Sue smiled at the memory of the three of them doing karaoke at the local pub on the Sunday evening before they wished Delia good luck with the interview. She also remembered how sad Delia had been when she talked about moving home as she really had thought that Jack was 'the one'.

That was a long time ago now and needless to say Delia was offered the job in

Willington and accepted it. Her Mum and Dad were more than glad to have her living at home again with them when she told them about the move.

Sue always remembers Delia's Mum telling her how sad Delia looked when she told them that she had been offered a super job and was moving back home.

Sue was looking at the time, and beginning to get anxious that she hadn't heard from Delia. She would sort out the children's tea in the next half hour if Neil hadn't come home. When he went on an emergency call out he could be ages. They may have to eat later once the children were sorted and she had heard from Delia.

Sue shouted the children to ask what sort of pizza's they wanted and she would order them from the nearby pizza place. She made the order and got the children to get plates and cutlery out just as Neil came in.

"Oh my goodness" exclaimed Sue when she saw the state of Neil. He was absolutely filthy from having to go into a cellar to sort out a leak.

"Go and get showered right away and get those clothes in the washer" said Sue, "I'm going to collect pizzas for the children".

"Hello kids" said Neil as he noted that Maisie and Joe were there. He looked enquiringly at Sue.

"Don't ask" whispered Sue, "I'll explain later" and with that she popped her coat on and went to get the pizzas whilst Neil did as his wife had instructed and went for a shower.

****

Both Val and Delia knew that Sue would always marry Neil as they had been sweethearts since High School. Sue started 'going out' with Neil when she was fourteen in year 9 and Neil was in year 11. It was no surprise to them when they got married soon after Sue finished college. They were devoted to each other and rarely ‘fell out’ and it was a delight to them all that they remained the best of friends.

Chapter 8

Whilst the children were sitting at the table munching on their pizzas, Sue summoned Neil to the kitchen so that they could talk without being overheard.

"Not that I mind Joe and Maisie being here, but I don't remember anything about it" said Neil.

"No, it wasn't planned" replied Sue. "As I was going to collect the children I had a call from Delia saying that Jack had been in an accident and was on her way to the hospital, and could I collect the children. So naturally I said I would. I asked her to ring as soon as she knew anything. She didn't phone while I was out did she?" asked Sue.

"No one's phoned Sue" said Neil, clearly alarmed at what Sue had told him.

"What time did she phone?" he asked.

"Well a minute before I went out to school. I asked her to phone as soon as she knew anything – but that is more than three hours ago" said Sue, starting to feel alarmed.

"Do you think we should try ringing her, Neil?"

"No. Lets give it another half an hour before we do that" replied Neil.

"I'm just concerned that the children are going to start asking questions if neither Delia or Jack doesn't come to pick them up soon" said Sue.

"We can occupy them for half an hour Sue," said Neil, "and we'll try and fob them off if there's a problem".

No sooner were the words out of Neil's mouth than they heard an almighty wail from the dining room.

They both moved very quickly to find Maisie and Joe having a fight over the last piece of pizza.

"It's mine Maisie", shouted Joe at her.

"You ate some of mine" yelled Maisie back.

"Now, now you two" said Neil soothingly.

"Shall we see if we can find some pudding instead of fighting over pizza" asked Sue.

Hostilities ceased immediately when the word 'pudding' was mentioned! Sue found them all suitable ice cream and the falling out over the pizza was soon forgotten.

Just as the children had returned to the dining room the phone rang. Sue picked it up and heard Delia's voice: "Sue".

"Delia, are you ok? How's Jack?" asked Sue taking the phone into the kitchen and closing the door so that the children couldn't hear. Sue knew from Delia's voice that she was distressed.

"Sue, it's not good" and Delia started to cry....

"Delia, tell me what's happened" asked Sue as Neil quietly came into the kitchen.

Slowly through her tears, Delia started to tell Sue that Jack had been in a head on car crash with a stolen car that the police were pursuing. It appeared that the driver was under age, high on drugs and had stolen a car to 'joy ride'!

No joy there, thought Sue as Delia paused to calm herself.

"Jack has got some really serious injuries – a broken leg, cracked sternam and he's in theatre now. They're operating as he seems to have some internal injuries"... Delia had started crying again and was sobbing as Sue started to cry with her.

Sue went back to that weekend when Delia thought there was no future for her and Jack . Having accepted the job offer in Willington she travelled back to the North East ready to hand in her notice and prepare to move back home in about a month. She would have to give at least a months notice on her flat and she would have to work about a month, unless they would let her take her holiday entitlement.

When she got back to her flat late on the Tuesday evening her answer machine was flashing signalling that there was a message. Delia kicked off her shoes, put the kettle on and pressed the answering machine messages.

“Delia, it’s Jack....... Where on earth are you? I’ve been trying to get hold of you all weekend but you’ve not answered my calls or emails”.

Click.

Another message.

“Delia.... It’s Jack... Again. WHERE ARE YOU?”

Click.

Another message.

“Delia.....It’s me...again......Jack......Please will you call me!”

Click.

Another message.

“Delia..... Jack,.....please will you CALL ME. I am worried sick. WHERE ARE YOU?”

The kettle had boiled so Delia made herself a cup of tea as she thought about the messages. It was too late really to call Jack now, and it was going to be a difficult conversation when she did speak to him.

She didn’t want to break up with him, but she knew that if she were to marry Jack, his mother would interfere and it would cause tension that would come between them.

Just as she was finishing her drink the phone rang, and as she had switched off the answer machine it continued to ring. Delia thought it might be her Mum making sure that she had got home safely so she answered it.

“Where on earth have you been.... I’ve been out of my mind with worry” , it was Jack.

As Delia was about to speak Jack said “Do not say a word. I am coming round NOW!”

Before Delia could respond the phone went dead, and she just looked at the

receiver in her hand.

Delia just had time to take her case into her bedroom and put the kettle on again when the doorbell rang.

Delia opened the door to find a very anxious Jack on the doorstep.

“Where on earth have you been, I’ve been out of my mind with worry” said Jack before Delia even had time to say hello!

“How about coming in Jack and then we can talk” said Delia.

Jack came in and took his coat off whilst Delia made them both drinks.

“I’ve been absolutely frantic” said Jack looking at Delia with very concerned eyes.

“What’s going on? Because I can tell that something is!”

“Well” said Delia. “You knew that I was meeting Sue and Val about the dresses for Sue’s wedding this weekend”.

“Yes - but you didn’t say that you were going to be away for a few days” interrupted Jack.

“Let me finish” said Delia quietly” and I’ll explain”.

Over the next ten minutes or so Delia told Jack how much she loved him but couldn't see a future for them, and honestly explained that she felt his mother would destroy their relationship. Because this had been bothering her for some weeks, and because his mother had scuppered several of their planned outings she felt that she should move away and as such had secured another job nearer home – her parent's home.

Jack listened quietly and patiently turning paler the more she explained. Delia wasn't one for scenes or shouting, she quietly explained her decision.

When Delia had finished, Jack sat very quietly looking at the floor then fished in his pocket for something. Pulling out a ring case and falling onto one knee he asked Delia to marry him.

"I've had the ring for weeks but wasn't sure how you would feel" said Jack. "Please say yes, Delia. I love you with all my heart, and we are right together – soul mates."

Delia was in a state of shock, but managed to shake her head.

"I do love you Jack, and nothing would make me happier – but I think your Mum would come between us, and I don't want that to happen..... for either of us" said Delia between the tears that were now freely running down her face.

" What if I were to tell you that I have been offered a job as the regional manager of that big chemist group in Willington?" said Jack.

"Willington?" said Delia puzzled.

"Yes" responded Jack, "Willington..... your Willington".

"Oh my goodness" was all Delia could say.

"And I've made it quite clear to my mother over the weekend that her phoning up and expecting me to drop everything has to stop! It would seem that even my Dad has told her as well! I knew what she was doing Delia, but after last week's little debacle I decided that she had gone far enough. I know you were disappointed that she had spoiled our day out – and it wasn't anything important.

I've been thinking about it all week, but because we've both been working late, I haven't had time to talk to you. I was going to ask you to marry me before you went to see the girlies but thought you would want it to be Sue's wedding time this weekend.

When you didn't get back last night I was worried out of my mind.... You didn't tell me that you were staying until today".

Delia's eyes filled with tears.

"Do you really mean that you would move to Willington for me?" asked Delia.

"No" said Jack..... "I'd move to Willington for US you silly girl".

"And you've really told your mother about interfering?" asked Delia.

"I have" replied Jack "and I've also told her that I want to marry you and move to Willington .... and she didn't have a heart attack" said Jack "in fact she rang me today to say that she was sorry for what she had done, and hoped we would be very happy........... So what do you say Delia Smith..... Will you marry me?"

Delia laughed out loud.... Jack always called her Delia Smith even though her name Morris, but he also knew that she liked baking cakes!

Between her laughter and tears Delia managed to say "Yes please".

"Ground to Sue".... Said Neil as Sue was clutching the phone listening to Delia's sobs at the other end.

Neil took the phone from Sue.

"Delia, it's Neil here..... Now, we need to be practical here. What can we do? What needs to be done?"

Delia managed to calm herself down whilst Neil put the phone on loud speaker.

"I'm not sure what to do, Neil, to be honest" said Delia. "Jack could be in surgery for some time and I don't really want to leave until I know the situation clearly".

"Ok" chipped in Sue "how about we keep the kids here for tonight? We will have to tell them something but we don't want to alarm them – any suggestions Delia?"

"We could say that your car has broken down and it will be late when you get home"

suggested Neil.

"Are you sure you don't mind, that would be really helpful" said Delia with relief in her voice.

"Look Delia" said Neil, "you shouldn't stay there all night. If Jack is bad and needs your support you are going to need some rest yourself. Shall I ring Val and Rupert and see about Rupert bringing me to the hospital and I'll drive you here?"

"Oh dear, I just don't know what to say – I should really contact Jack's mother in case anything happens," and Delia started to sob again.

"Delia, listen. Keep your phone close at hand and Sue and I will think through what needs to be done, but we'll get the children sorted out first" said Neil. "In the meantime, if you need us call immediately, otherwise we'll speak to you in about an hour".

Neil looked at Sue, clearly as worried as she was.

"First things first, we need to sort out the children and we don't want to alarm them. Give your face a wash Sue or they'll realise you've been crying" said Neil, practical as ever.

Not a moment too soon after Sue had cleared her head, the bell rang and there was Joyce delivering Adam home after his visit with Steven.

“Home safe and sound” announced Joyce with a beaming smile.

Adam came in after thanking Joyce for his tea and bringing him home. As Adam made his way into the house Joyce said to Sue quietly

“ What’s this I’ve been hearing about Alice and Brian, It’s not true is it?“

Neil looked at Sue and said “why, what’s happened with Brian and Alice?”

Sue realised that with everything going on with Delia she hadn’t had time to tell Neil what she had heard.

“I don’t know Joyce” replied Sue..... “Neil, I’ll tell you what I’ve heard later”.

“For the time being Joyce, if you hear anything, please will you just damp it down until we really know what’s happened. If there is a problem, then we need to be there to support Brian, don’t you agree?”

“Well, yes, absolutely” replied Joyce.

“When I know anything definite I will let you know – but for the time being, I think we should keep the gossiping to a minimum” stated Sue.

“That’s fine Sue, I’ll not repeat what has been said” replied Joyce. “Anyway, I need to get a move on or I’ll have Laura hopping up and down on the school steps”.

Chapter 9

The house that Sue and Neil had bought soon after they were married was in a rather dilapidated state, but there was definite potential for extending as there was a lot of ground at the side and a big garden at the rear. Over time they had worked hard to extend so that they had a large family house with a bedroom each for the children, an office and a spare bedroom for visitors...... Or if Neil was in the 'dog house', he used to say to friends laughing!

Neil had worked hard to build up his business and Sue was always there supporting him and he felt that this lovely house was Sue's reward for putting up with all sorts of mess and long working hours at the beginning.

The children each had beds with a pull out bed underneath so that they could have their friends to stay without disruption. Sue and Neil were very easy going and enjoyed the delight that their children felt when they had friends over.

It made it so much easier tonight when Delia's children needed to stay .

By the time the two younger boys were bathed and in bed asleep and the two girls were in bed reading, Rupert and Val had arrived.

Sue had explained to the children that there was a problem with Jack's car and so they could have a sleep over tonight. The mention of a sleep over brought squeals of joy – they always enjoyed 'sleep overs', they thought it meant that they could stay up late! Not on this occasion explained Sue, as it was school the following day!

Quickly, but reluctantly the children settled .

Adam couldn't work our what was happening when Val & Rupert arrived but suspected that something was amiss.

"Mum, what's going on?" asked Adam.

“There’s a bit of a problem with Uncle Jack’s car” explained Sue “and we need to go into ’Musketeer’ mode”.

This always made the children laugh. Neil had regularly called the three ’girls’, as he called them, the Musketeers whenever they were doing something together.

Whilst Adam played on his games console before going to bed, Sue ushered Val & Rupert into the kitchen where Neil had already boiled the kettle.

“Do you know how bad the situation is” asked Val.

“Not really” replied Neil. “Delia was so upset she couldn’t really explain what has happened, other than to say that Jack was in theatre being operated on”.

“I wasn’t going to come” said Val, “as I was feeling a bit rough earlier on – but as I feel ok now I though that if you want to go with the guys, I’ll stay and babysit and you can perhaps persuade Delia to come home and get some rest. But whatever she decides , it gives her some options”.

“Hmm,” said Sue “you’re probably right. Would you prefer to go and I’ll stay here?”

“Whilst you were getting the kids sorted out for bed” said Neil to Sue “we decided that we should go to the hospital so that if Delia wants to come back one of us would drive her car, as we didn’t think she’d be in any fit state to drive”.

“I would prefer that Val stayed here, if you don’t mind Sue. She was out for the count when I got home, and if she’s coming down with something it would best if she stayed away from hospitals!” exclaimed Rupert.

“If you’re sure Val, that you don’t mind staying, then I’ll be glad to go and see what has happened.” replied Sue.

“That’s absolutely fine with me” said Val. At that moment Adam popped his nose in the kitchen.

“Auntie Val..... I didn’t know you were here” going straight to Val and giving her a hug.

Val was Adam’s Godmother along with Delia and Val adored him.

“Hello my lovely godson. Isn’t it your bedtime yet?” she said with a smile on her face.

“I think we need to get going” said Neil.

“Can I stay up a little bit longer and have a game of cards with Auntie Val” asked Adam to either of his parents.

“It’s up to Auntie Val” said Sue, knowing full well that Val would play with him all night if she could. Looking at Val as she nodded Sue said.... “well OK, but only half an hour – it’s school tomorrow”.

“Thanks Mum” replied Adam as he gave her a hug. With that he went in search of some cards.

As Neil, Rupert and Sue got their coats on Val asked with concern in her voice, “Will you ring me and let me know what’s going on as soon as you can?”

In unison they all said “yes of course”, and with that they quietly went out through the front door hoping not to disturb the sleeping children.

Chapter 10

During the half hour journey when Rupert drove them to the hospital, Sue updated Neil and Rupert on what Delia had told her and Val that morning about Alice being seen leaving the vicarage.

“I find that really hard to take in” said Rupert. “I know I don’t know them as well as you two, but they always seem so happy when you see them together. Are you sure Delia had the story right?”

“Well one thing I know about Delia,” said Neil “she is very accurate with everything she does – meticulous, but she was repeating what had been said to her and if the gossipers are adding little bits every time the story is told it could be way off mark”.

“If what we’ve heard is true” said Sue, “we will need to be there to support Brian. I emailed him earlier to let him know we were thinking about him and here for him when he’s ready – or if he needs anything. What we don’t want to do is intrude....... He will be feeling dreadful if all this is accurate.”

Both Neil and Rupert agreed and Sue knew that they would give whatever support was needed, just as she knew it would be the case this evening with Jack and Val as they entered the hospital car park.

As it was late they had been able to park fairly close to the main entrance and they made their way quickly to find Delia. As there was no one about Sue phoned Delia who answered immediately and gave them directions to where she was waiting.

Delia heard the three of them as soon as they entered the corridor and she shot up and ran to them as she couldn't contain the tears any longer. Delia was anguished and Sue started to cry when she saw how desperate her friend was. Sue hugged Delia tightly until the crying subsided.

Neil was the first to speak.." Have you heard any more from the doctors Delia?"

Delia shook her head finding it hard to speak, but managed to say, "No..... The nurse said that someone would come to me when he came out of theatre, but that was hours ago" as she started to cry again.

"Have you had anything to eat or drink?" asked Sue.

"Oh, I couldn't eat anything" said Delia, "I just feel sick"!

"Well I think we should all have a drink" stated Rupert. "It could be some time before we know anything. I'll go in search of teas and coffee. Neil, can you help me with them?"

"Yes, of course. We won't be long you two." said Neil as he gave Delia a hug .

As the two men went in search of drinks, Delia turned to Sue, "What did you tell the children?" she asked anxiously.

"Don't worry" said Sue taking Delia's hand. "We told them that there was a problem with the car and you would be late back. They're fine! They had pizza for tea – which I understand is Joe's favourite and he was looking forward to it tonight! And the idea of a sleep-over was very exciting – so no problem, don't worry".

"Now, tell me..... what do you know about the accident, and what have the police said to you?" asked Sue.

Delia took a deep breath and gathered her thoughts.

"All I can gather at the moment is that the police were in pursuit of a stolen car with a young lad at the wheel. He rounded the bend on that narrow road off the Willchester by-pass and lost control – straight into Jack's car ."

Delia was visibly shaking now and the tears were running down her face.

"What am I going to do without him Sue?" she sobbed.

Taking command Sue said, "Now you can stop that right away. We don't know how bad it is until we speak to the doctors, and until we know, we all must stay strong".

"Who needs to stay strong?" said Neil coming back with Rupert and the drinks.

"I was just telling Delia, that she mustn't think the worst – we need to hear what the doctors have to say" replied Sue.

"I think Sue's right" said Rupert gently. "Let's try to stay positive until we know exactly what the situation is",

As the four of them sat quietly drinking tea in cardboard cartons, two police officers came along the corridor.

"Mrs. Harris?" asked one of the police officers.

Delia immediately got up spilling some of the hot tea on her coat...

"Yes. I'm Mrs. Harris. What's wrong. Have you heard something?" Delia stuttered.

"No, Mrs. Harris. We came to see if you were alright and to see how your husband is doing. I'm glad to see that you have someone with you. The driver of the stolen car is under arrest".

"Is he alright?" Delia asked the police officer.

"Well he has quite a few injuries – to be honest I don't know how he got out alive, but he will certainly be going down for this. He is known to us and under investigation for other crimes as well ." replied the officer.

"Anyway, as long as you have someone with you, we'll leave you in peace. Here's my card with my direct phone number. Should you need me at all please ring. We will be in touch with you tomorrow. If you get chance, ring me and let me know when your husband is out of surgery - I'm on duty all night tonight, so you won't be disturbing me.... and I would really like to know how your husband is ".

With that the two officers departed leaving the four friends drinking their somewhat colder stewed tea!

Neil was the first to speak. "He seemed a pretty decent chap that policeman .... I wonder what else the little devil is under investigation for...."

"Well whatever it is, it sounds as if he isn't going anywhere at the moment" replied Rupert.

Delia got up suddenly and started pacing up and down. "I can't stand this waiting " she cried, "Why doesn't someone let us know what's happening?"

Sue went to her and tried to comfort her . She had never seen her friend so frantic. Delia was always in control and to see her so anguished was almost more than she could bare.

Neil got up and said "I'll go and see if I can find anything out, I thought we might have had some news by now."

"I'll stay with the girls", said Rupert, "Just in case someone turns up". Neil looked at Rupert with a knowing nod........ They were all starting to think the worst.

A few minutes after Neil had gone looking for a nurse Rupert's phone rang. He looked at Sue and Delia... "It's ok, it's Val. She probably wants to know what's going on," he said as he

answered the call.

He explained to Val what was going on and Sue asked if she could have a word.

Rupert passed the phone to Sue. "Hi Val, have the children settled ok?" asked Sue.

"They're fine" replied Val, "all asleep. Is Delia within earshot?"

"No" replied Sue.

"Ok. So... Can you tell me the situation?" asked Val

"It's a bit difficult.... Neil's gone looking for a nurse or doctor as we've been here a couple of hours now and heard nothing." replied Sue.

"It sounds very bad Sue" said Val.

"Hmmm, it's difficult" was Sue's response.

"I understand.... Delia would overhear?" asked Val.

"Yes, I think so" answered Sue.

"One word answers then" asked Val

"Ok" said Sue, "I think I can do that".

"Do you know what happened and how bad is it looking?" asked Val.

"Well the police were here a little while ago. They have arrested the 'boy' who was driving—it seems he was being pursued by a police car – stolen car etc. And he's known to the police. He has also got serious injuries, but not as bad as Jack, it would seem."

"I take it that it's not looking good for Jack then?" asked Val.

"Not at the moment" replied Sue lowering her voice." As soon as we hear anything we'll give you a call."

As Sue handed the phone back to Rupert a doctor came into view walking alongside Neil.

"Mrs. Harris?" asked the doctor looking from Delia to Sue.

"Yes . I'm Mrs. Harris" said Delia visibly shaking. Sue took hold of her hand as the doctor indicated that they should sit .

"I'm Dr Clark and I've just come from theatre." He could see that Delia was shaking and he took hold of her hand.

"Your husband is on his way to ICU. We've had to remove his spleen , repair a broken leg and broken wrist and he's got a couple of broken ribs. He's very lucky it wasn't worse – the size of the car saved him..... The next twenty four hours is crucial as he'll be suffering from shock as well as being in pain when he comes round."

Delia was already crying and Sue was having difficulty containing the tears.

"When can I see him?" asked Delia.

"He is sedated at the moment so he wouldn't know you were there" replied the doctor.

"Please, I just need to see him" said Delia, tears flowing now.

The doctor hesitated....... "You may get a shock when you see him as he's got tubes all over and as I said he is sedated ..... Do you think you could mange seeing him like that?"

"I just need to see him" repeated Delia.

The doctor looked at the three very concerned friends as Neil very gently nodded to him.

"Well let me go and see whether he's now comfortable in ICU and once he is I will come and collect you – but I want you to promise me that once you've seen him you will go home and get some sleep as I'm sure that the next few days will be very stressful for you."

Delia nodded in agreement "thank you, thank you doctor for everything".

The doctor smiled at them all and nodded and went to see how Jack was.

Both Rupert and Neil looked relieved that Jack had come through the operation and Neil gave Delia a big hug as she stood up. She had managed to stop crying and she was only shaking a little now.

Delia looked at her watch and realised how long her friends had been with her.

"Oh my goodness, you need to get home, you've got work in the morning" exclaimed Delia.

"I think work is the last thing on any of our minds at present" said Rupert now giving Delia a hug. "As it's so late I think the best thing we can do is for Neil to drive your car back to their house."

"Absolutely" said Sue "the spare bed is made up for you anyway, and I'll get the children to school in the morning".

Delia hadn't got the energy to argue and was relieved that she didn't have to think too much at the moment.

A few minutes later Dr Clark came back. "Mrs. Harris, you can see your husband now – but only for five minutes – no longer! He's very drowsy and we'll be sedating him again shortly so don't worry if he's not sure who you are."

"Neil are you ok to bring Delia in her car?" asked Rupert as Delia walked away with the doctor.

"Yes that's fine" replied Neil "Why?"

"I think I should take Sue so that she can make sure everything is OK with the children and we can explain to Val before Delia gets back."

"That's a very good idea" said Neil. "I'm sure we won't be far behind you. Drive carefully!"

He gave Sue a quick kiss "I'll see you soon" and went to catch up with Delia and the doctor.

"Let's get going" said Sue to Rupert "I bet Val's fast asleep on the settee" she said with a little laugh trying to lighten the intense worry that they both felt.

"Either that or she'll be watching some late night film" chortled Rupert.

It was well past midnight when they got out of the hospital and quite cool for a spring evening. Rupert's car was a big 'posh' one and the heater soon warmed up.

As they got out of the hospital grounds Sue said to Rupert : "I wonder what investigation the police are doing with the boy they've arrested."

"Well for starters he stole the car that was involved tonight, but I must say that police chap did say there was something else they were looking into . We may get to know more tomorrow . I just hope that Jack gets through the night without complications."

The roads were quiet and Rupert got them back quite quickly.

Sue went in very quietly to find Val fast asleep on the sofa. She smiled as she looked at her friend and Rupert gently stroked her hair saying "wake up sleepy head"!

Val gave a little moan and then realised where she was and was almost instantly awake.

"Oh my goodness – what time is it?"

"Late, very late" replied Sue.

"Where's Neil and Delia?" asked Val.......

For the next ten minutes they told Val all that they knew and that the next twenty four hours were crucial.

They had just finished updating Val and she gathered her things together ready to go as Neil and Delia walked in. Delia looked grey and drained and Val gave her a big bear hug.

"I saw him for a few minutes" Delia told them all. "He's hooked up to lines and wires and goodness knows what, but the nurse said that after an operation it's normal. I didn't want to leave him" she said as she tried to keep the tears inside. "They will know more tomorrow and they said that I could ring anytime."

"I think we should all try to get some sleep – you look washed out Val. Are you OK?" asked Sue.

"Yes. I was a bit off this afternoon. I'm tired, so I agree we all need sleep. We'll ring you in the morning but if you need us, or anything, just phone." said Val as Rupert gathered her things together.

"Night everyone" said Val & Rupert in unison. "And Delia.....try not to worry. You'll need your strength when Jack gets home." said Val.

As Val and Rupert left, Delia made a quick call to the police officer who had left his number. She quickly update him and he said he would speak to her later on when she had had some sleep.

Chapter 11

Despite having had little sleep, Sue and Neil were up for the children the following morning. Trying to get five children washed, dressed, breakfasted and ready for school following the trauma of the previous evening was nothing short of a circus! But somehow they did it.

Maisie and Joe wanted to know about their Mum & Dad so Sue explained that they had been very late back and that their Mum was still asleep in the spare room and to let her have a lie in. Reluctantly they did so but only on condition that they could peep at her before they went to school!

As it was Friday Delia would usually pick them up as she finished work early, so Sue assured the children that she would pick them up from school at the end of the day.

As Sue got to the school gates she could see a group of mums talking quite animatedly. She didn't really give it much thought until she got nearer and overheard their conversation.

She heard Bev, one of the mums with a child the same age as Flora say "I'm telling you she's gone! It's all over the village."

Sue groaned inwardly. She hadn't even thought about Alice and Brian since they entered the hospital last night and she knew what was coming!

"Here's Sue now...She's bound to know what's going on" said another mum.

"Bye Mum" shouted Adam to Sue as he met his friend in the playground. "See you later."

"OK love. Have a good day" shouted Sue back as she ushered Flora, Bobby, Maisie and Joe into school.

Sue desperately wanted to avoid any questioning about Brian and Alice. She didn't know anything anyway! But could she escape – not a chance! They were on her like a pack of wolves wanting to know about the gossip they had heard.

"Look" said Sue to about half a dozen mums who had descended on her, "I don't know anything ."

"I find that hard to believe" said one of the surly mums she always avoided. "You are the churchwarden after all!"

"I may be churchwarden" replied Sue, "But the private life of our vicar and his wife is exactly that : PRIVATE" she said trying to stay calm. Sue did not want to get into an argument with anyone and as this was just food for gossip she wanted to avoid it at all costs. She was also very keen to get back to Delia so that she could phone the hospital to check on Jack.

"Now if you'll excuse me I have things to do, and it would be appreciated if this gossip stopped here as it really isn't helpful and Brian has been very kind to several of you" looking directly at the surly mum who Brian had helped by providing food when her husband left! With that Sue turned and walked swiftly home. As Sue walked through the door Delia was coming downstairs wearing Sue's dressing gown.

"Oh my goodness" said Delia "look at the time. You should have woken me!"

"You needed your sleep" replied Sue.

"What about the children" asked Delia.

"What about them" laughed Sue...... "they've all had breakfast, were washed and dressed and ready for school without fuss..... Unbelievably" mused Sue. "Maisie and Joe did want to see you" continued Sue "so I let then have a little peep at you asleep before taking them to school".

"Oh Sue... I don't know how I would have managed without you yesterday.. And today" said Delia eyes filling with tears again.

"Now stop that" said Sue "we need to put a plan in place so that you can visit Jack and we can organise the children".

"Oh no" said Delia suddenly very alarmed and putting her hands to her face.

"What's the matter" said Sue taking hold of Delia's hands.

"I haven't phoned Jack's Mum – she'll be frantic when she knows and also want to know why I didn't ring her last night" responded Delia. "You know what she can be like, Sue. I still feel that she thinks I stole her son away from her!"

" Well you can stop talking rubbish right away! She couldn't have done anything last night even if she had known, and to be honest, she would have been constantly ringing and that would not have been particularly helpful would it?"

Delia shook her head knowing that what Sue had said was true. She sat down heavily with her head in her hands. "What am I going to do"?

"I'll tell you what you're going to do" said Sue. "You can start by ringing the hospital NOW and finding out how Jack is and what sort of night he's had – then you're going to have a shower while I make us both some breakfast, and then we'll start putting a plan together. How does that sound?"

Delia took a deep a deep breath as Sue handed her the phone. "Yes. OK."

Delia phoned the hospital and waited only a couple of minutes before she was put through to the ICU where she had seen Jack the night before.

The nurse told her that Jack had had a comfortable night and that the doctor would be there to see him in the next hour or so and if she wanted to ring back then she may be able to give her some more information.

Delia thanked her and said that she would ring back later .

Sue insisted that Delia had a shower and got herself dressed before they did anything else.

Delia agreed and as she went upstairs Sue started to sort out breakfast. Sue felt this could be a long day so she decided to do a cooked breakfast which would keep them going. Neil had left for work just before she had taken the children to school and although he told her to ring him if they needed him, Sue didn't expect to see him before later that afternoon, so it was a surprise when he walked through the door as she was organising toast.

"Well this is a surprise" said Sue to her husband. "Is everything alright".

"Yes" said Neil. "I went out without one of my tool bags – I think everything that happened last night was on my mind. Anyway, I'm only at Mrs. Snape's at the end of the Village, so I thought I'd just pop back and pick it up. How's Delia this morning"?

Well she's phoned the hospital and they said that Jack has had a comfortable night – whatever comfortable really means! She's concerned that she didn't let Jack's mother know last night. But if she had there wouldn't have been anything she could have done"replied Sue.

"I'm making us a cooked breakfast as we don't really know what the day ahead may bring. Do you want something while you're here?" Sue asked Neil.

"I wouldn't mind a quick bacon butty if you've got enough on the go" said Neil.

Sue set to and buttered bread ready to put lashings of bacon on and silently thanking God that she had Neil, and at the same time asking him to heal Jack.

Sue smiled to herself as she often prayed quietly when she was doing jobs around the house. She had a very strong faith but wasn't pious and never 'threw' her religion or faith at people. She tried hard to just do her best whenever and wherever she could.

As Sue finished layering the bacon onto the bread for Neil, Delia came downstairs and joined them.

“Good morning” said Neil “and how do you feel today?”

“Good morning Neil – I hope I haven’t delayed you?” asked Delia

“No, not at all. I forgot a tool bag so came back for it. I’m only working at the end of the village.... But I’m glad I did as I’ve bagged myself a bacon butty!” laughed Neil as Sue wrapped it in foil for him to take.

“Lovely.. thanks Sue” said Neil giving her a kiss. “I’ll see you later, but don’t forget if you need me at all, just give me a ring. And Delia...... Try not to worry”. Delia nodded and with that Neil made himself scarce.

Sue and Delia sat down to breakfast and Sue had a notepad and pen in hand ready to start a plan.

Delia hadn’t eaten since the day before and suddenly realised how hungry she was.

“I didn’t think I would be able to eat anything” said Delia “but I now realise that I am ravenous!”

“We need to make sure that we’ve got fuel in us today as we don’t know where we will have to go, or what we will have to do” replied Sue.

Now on their second cup of tea, Sue said ”Ok. We need to make a list. Where shall we start?”

Delia paused for a moment and looked at the time. “Do you think it would be too soon to ring the hospital again? I’d like to have a clearer idea of how bad Jack is before I ring his mother.”

“It’s over an hour since you rang” said Sue “So you could give it a try. The more information you have the better” and Sue went to get the phone.

Luckily Delia got through very quickly again. The nurse she had spoken to earlier answered the phone and told her that the doctor was with Jack now and she would get him to the phone. It was Dr Clark who spoke to her – the doctor she had seen the night before.

"Hello Mrs. Harris . I hope you managed to get some rest last night" enquired the doctor.

Somewhat unexpectedly I did, thank you Doctor." replied Delia . "How is my husband this morning?"

"I've just looked him over and he's had a reasonable night. He's still very drowsy due to the sedation but without it he would have been in a lot of pain. We're going to keep him in ICU for another 24 hours to keep an eye on him, but I think the danger has now passed. It's going to take him quite some time to recover however, but I think it's safe to say that he will make a full recovery." reported the doctor.

"Thank you, thank you so much" said Delia as she started to cry. "Is it ok to visit today?"

"Yes. That's fine" replied Dr Clark. "I would leave it until this afternoon so that we can tidy him up and top his pain killers up as well. He may be drowsy when you come, and I wouldn't advise that you stay for very long today. But I understand that you want to see him. If you need anything else from me, just let the sister on the ward know and I will get back to you. Try not to worry too much" said the doctor and after saying goodbye they hung up.

Chapter 12

Having got an update from the hospital Sue advised Delia to ring Jack's mother before they did anything else. Delia agreed knowing that it wasn't going to be an easy conversation.

Sue left Delia to phone her mother-in-law and went to check her email. As soon as she opened her email she saw one from Brian and immediately felt guilty as she had completely forgotten about the situation with Alice with everything that had happened last night. Sue opened the email and read Brian's email. He told her that he was ok and that he assumed she had heard the gossip, that he couldn't talk about it at present but hoped that everything would work out alright. He told her that he appreciated her support and would have a proper conversation with her as soon as he could.

Sue sent a quick reply telling him that both Neil and herself were here for him if he needed anything. Just before she clicked send she thought it best to tell him about Jack. Brian knew Jack as he supported most of the church events even though he was only an infrequent church attendee.

Whilst Sue was still checking her emails one came straight back from Brian saying how sorry he was to hear about Jack and offered his help and support along with his prayers. He asked to be kept updated as to his progress and also said that he would visit him once he was on a main ward.

Sue was deeply touched by his quick response especially with everything he was dealing with at the moment and she thought that Delia would appreciate it too.

Just as she sent a quick thank you reply Delia appeared at the study door.

“How did it go?” asked Sue looking at the tortured face of her friend.

“It could have been worse” said Delia. “You know what she’s like – almost hysterical when I told her and demanded to know why I hadn’t phoned last night. I explained how late it was when we got back and we weren’t sure of his injuries until this morning. Of course she wanted all the ins and outs of the crash and I couldn’t tell her because I don’t know myself. Anyway, she calmed down a little when I told her what the doctor had told us this morning. But of course, she’s demanding to come down! ”

“That’s all you need” piped in Sue “doesn’t she realise how stressful this is for you, and you will have to tell the children later.”

“Oh my, I had almost forgotten that. You’re right Sue – the children are going to want to know where their daddy is this evening. I’m not sure that I’ve actually put her off. She was going to ring Jack’s sister to tell her then call back.”

“Let’s have a coffee and work out the nest step” said Sue.

Back in the kitchen Sue and Delia came up with a plan for telling the children after school. They would all come back to Sue’s for tea and then see how the children felt about another sleep over. This would give Delia some time to go home and get items that Jack would need in hospital and also give her a little bit of breathing space.

As they were about to leave the house Delia’s phone rang. It was Jack’s sister Diane.

“Delia, I’ve just had Mum on the phone saying that Jack’s been in an accident. She’s

frantic and I couldn’t make it all out, except to say that she’s looking at train times to come down to you! What has happened?”

"Hello Diane" replied Delia who then told her as much as she knew.

"Oh you poor thing" sympathised Diane. "It would be easier if I could put mother off coming down at the moment, wouldn't it?"

"Well to be honest Diane, yes it would. It's not that I don't want her to come but Jack is still in ICU and the children don't know yet – it was too late last night and they were fast asleep. The police will also have to interview him when he's feeling up to it. They have arrested someone, but Jack will still need to give a statement" explained Delia. "I also have quite a bit of running around to do today as I need to speak to people at work and I want to get to the hospital early this afternoon so that I'm back to collect the children from school".

"I will do my best Delia, to put her off – but no promises – she can be very strong willed when she puts her mind to it" and both Diane and Delia laughed. "I'll speak to you later once you've been to the hospital so that you can update me. In the meantime, look after yourself and try not to worry too much" ended Diane.

Sue had heard all the conversation and was shaking her head. "Does that woman not realise the strain that you are under" she asked Delia.

"Jack is her son Sue, you know the reference :'this is my beloved son'! Well that's Jack's Mum. I know she will want to come down, I just hope she gives me a couple of days to get my head round what has happened and tell the children."

Sue and Delia picked up their bags about to leave for a second time when Sue's phone started to ring. They both looked at one another and Sue was about to ignore it until she saw that the caller was Val.

"Good morning my friend, and how are you this morning? You looked completely done in last night – but thanks for sitting with the children anyway" opened Sue.

"Hello you two – that is I'm assuming that Delia is still with you?" answered Val.

"Yes, I'm here " called Delia "You're on loudspeaker so we can all talk.

"How's Jack this morning – have you heard from the hospital?" asked Val.

Delia updated her and said that once she had sorted out work she was going straight up to the hospital.

"If there's anything I can do just call – I'm working from home today, so I'll be easy to get hold of" said Val.

"Well actually" chirped in Sue "could you be available to pick the kids up from school if we get delayed".

"No problem, just ring me about fifteen minutes before if there is a problem, otherwise I'll ring you later on. Take care both of you" and with that Val hung up.

"Delia... I think we should go and get things for Jack from your house and then we can go straight to the hospital later on.... What do you think?" asked Sue.

"Yes, I think you're probably right." replied Delia. "I'm a bit concerned that Jack's mother will be planning her visitation! In which case I'll have to sort out the bedrooms etcetera! If there's a speck of dust in the place,she'll comment!"

"Don't you think it's time you put that woman straight?" responded Sue "You've let her irritate you for a long time – Jack made it clear a long time ago that she wasn't to interfere..... So don't let her get to you now. It's time she realised how accommodating you are and that she should take you as she finds you. Especially at the moment – she should be thinking about Jack getting well and how you will cope."

“I know Sue, but she always seems to intimidate me” replied Delia sadly.

Delia would have liked nothing more than to have a good relationship with her mother in law, but Betty (Jack’s Mum) had never been very warm to her.

Sue put her arm round Delia..... “Well it’s her loss – she could have such a friend in you if only she realised” said Sue. “Anyway, come on we’ve got lots to do today so I think we should make a start.”

Chapter 13

Sue said that she would drive and they started off by going to Delia's first of all. They put a bag of essentials together to take to the hospital for Jack and Delia checked her emails and answer machine. There were a couple of messages that she needed to respond to so whilst she did this and contacted Jack's boss to tell him what had happened, Sue attacked the crockery that had been left in the sink and generally tidied round the kitchen making them some lunch at the same time. They were just having a sandwich before going to the hospital when Delia's phone rang. She looked at it and grimaced.

"It's Betty" Delia told Sue "shall I answer it or ignore it?"

"If you don't answer it she'll be ringing you all afternoon and then wanting to know *why* you didn't answer" replied Sue.

"Yes, you're right" said Delia as she answered the call.

Sue watched Delia's face go from pale to even paler and tears fill her eyes as she listened to Betty on the other end of the phone.

Delia was almost monosyllabic in her answers to Betty – largely because she couldn't get a word in edgeways! Sue was trying to tic tac to Delia to put her on loud speaker so she could hear what was going on. Delia did this just before the call came to an end.

It was clear from what Sue heard that she was ranting and raving about not being wanted. She had spoken to Diane who had tried to put her off visiting until Jack was improved and Betty went off at the deep end.

Delia put the phone down after trying to explain to Betty that of course she was welcome, but that Jack was still in ICU and the children didn't know about the accident yet.

It was clear that Betty was not going to listen to reason and the call was ended.

Delia was both angry and intimidated with her mother in law and the tears came forth and she could hardly stop.

Sue put her arm round her and rocked her until she became calm.

"That woman is an absolute menace. She is so selfish – she shows no compassion whatsoever. Did she actually ask how Jack was" asked Sue as Delia shook her head and dried her tears.

"Now look Delia, you must not let her keep doing this to you. You need to be strong for the children and for Jack. Get your things together, we need to make a move to the hospital otherwise we won't be back in time to collect the children."

Sue took the plates and cups into the kitchen and quickly washed them as Delia got everything together.

Ten minutes later they were in the car leaving for the hospital just as Delia's phone rang again. This time it was Diane.

"Hi Diane" said Delia "you OK?"

I am absolutely furious" raged Diane as she answered Delia "with my MOTHER! I told her specifically NOT to phone you until I had spoken to you after you had seen Jack today.... But no....mother being mother she has to put her two penath in.... I am so, so sorry Delia"..

As Diane paused for breath, and Delia's phone was on loud speaker Sue chipped in...

"Hi Diane, Sue here, we're just on our way to the hospital now. Diane, your mum is well out of order speaking to Delia the way she did. Does she have no understanding of the impact her behaviour has on Delia? She really is not being fair at all. I know I'm not family, but I see the impact of her words on Delia... and it's just not on!"

Before Delia could respond Diane said "Yes I know Sue, and I'm only thankful that you are there for Delia. I do understand what you are saying and I agree with you. I know that a lot of it is because she is worried – as we all are. When I've calmed down I will speak to her again.... I've actually walked out of her house as I was so angry with her!"

At that Delia started to laugh "are you sure you've done the right thing there Dee... she might ban you..." chipped in Delia.

"Well yes, she might for ten minutes, until she wants me to do something" replied Diane sarcastically . "Look Delia, I'm not going to let her get away with it.....she really has to learn that she can't keep behaving like this. I'll get back to you later.....give my love to Jack" and with that Diane hung up.

"I know I shouldn't have said anything" said Sue, "but I can't stand by anymore and let that woman walk all over you – even if she is Jack's mother".

Delia was quiet for a few minutes while Sue took care driving.

Eventually Delia said "I know that you are right Sue, but I just do not know how to handle her.... I've never been intimidated in this way....I can deal with people at work and when there's been issues at school I've never had a problem...... but this woman.." Delia tailed off.

"I know it's difficult Delia, but unless you find a way to be strong with her, she will come between you and Jack.... And we're not going to let that happen!"

By this time they were approaching the hospital and needed to find a place to park.

Delia took the bag with Jack's things in from the back seat and Sue got a parking ticket. Once inside they found their way to ICU and Delia asked to see Jack .

The nurse on duty said that he could only have one visitor at a time. Sue told Delia to go in and take as long as she wanted as she would wait outside where there were some chairs. Delia hugged her friend and went to see her husband.

Sue sat watching people pass by and reflected on the last twenty four hours. She couldn't quite get her head round how much had happened in that time. It was only yesterday that the three of them had been in their usual 'Mugs with Hugs' for their weekly get together and were struggling with the news that Alice had left Brian. How quickly things can change she pondered.

Before she realised over half an hour had passed and Delia came out of the ward.

Sue stood up to see a much more relieved Delia than when she had gone in.

"How is he" asked Sue. Delia's eyes filled with tears but nodded her head. "He'll be ok, but it will take a long time. He said to go in for a minute if you want. He's a bit drowsy now but would be happy to see you for a minute."

"OK" said Sue "I'll just pop in for a minute."

When Sue went in to the ward and saw Jack wired up with drips and other mechanical equipment she had to keep a grip on her emotions. She didn't want him or Delia to see her cry – she needed to be strong for her friends.

"Hi Jack" said Sue as he just raised his hand to wave to her. "How are you feeling?"

Jack nodded "Well I'm still here, thank God! How's Delia doing" he asked quietly.

"She's OK Jack – shocked, as we all are, but we're all here for you both – you know that." replied Sue.

"Sue, can I ask you something?" Jack said quietly.

"Of course– what is it?"

“ Don’t let Delia be intimidated by my mother. I know what she’s like and how rude she can be sometimes. Delia doesn’t need being upset by her at the moment. I know that she’s worried about me and that she needs to tell the children.” Jack looked at Sue intently.

“Don’t worry Jack. We’ll sort your mother out” laughed Sue and Jack had a little smile. “I’ve already spoken to Diane and she will keep your mother in check!”

“Thanks Sue.... I really appreciate it” said Jack.

Sue could see that he needed to rest. “Don’t worry about anything... Just get yourself better and we’ll see you soon.“

Sue blew him a kiss and went back to Delia in the corridor.

“What do you think” asked Delia , as soon as Sue came from the ward.

“I think he will be fine, but I think it will be weeks before he’s really well.” replied Sue as Delia nodded. Sue observed that she did look better than a few hours ago. Seeing Jack and being able to talk to him had made a huge difference to her but she still had to tell the children, and that was worrying her.

It started to rain as they walked back to the car park and they both huddled under Sue’s umbrella to avoid getting too wet. As they got in the car Delia’s phone rang. It wasn’t a number she recognised so she answered it a little bit tentatively.

“Is that Mrs. Harris” came the man’s voice “yes” responded Delia.

“It’s Sergeant Brooks here – I spoke to you last night in the hospital.”

“Oh yes” replied Delia “how are you?”

"More to the point Mrs. Harris, how are you and how is your husband today?" asked the policeman.

"I'm fine, thank you. My husband is still in ICU but they are looking to move him tomorrow all being well" Delia told him.

"Do you think we would be able to interview him once he's out of ICU Mrs. Harris?" asked the sergeant.

"I think that would probably be alright, as long as you don't tire him out too much. He does need rest at the moment, and will do for some time" Delia told him.

Thank you. I'll be in touch with you tomorrow and arrange a time. Would you like to be there when we see him?" asked the Sergeant.

"Yes, if that's possible" replied Delia.

"I think that will be fine. I'll let you know when we have a time arranged" and with that the Sergeant hung up.

Sue looked at the time as they drove out of the car park a little concerned that they might be pushing it to get back in time to collect the children from school.

"Do you think we should give Val a call and ask her to collect the children for us?" Sue asked Delia. "We could be a bit late if we get stuck in traffic or behind a tractor on the little roads...especially now that it's raining."

Delia looked at her watch. "Yes. I think it might be an idea."

With that she got her phone out and called Val who answered on the second ring.

"Hi you two. How's Jack doing?" Val asked immediately.

"He's very tired and full of pain killers, but he's on the mend, even though it will take some time." Delia told her.

"I must say Delia , you sound much better than earlier on....are you a bit happier now that you've seen him?" replied Val.

"Oh yes, absolutely." smiled Delia into the phone. "The only snag now is telling the children. And talking of children......which is really why I'm phoning....would you mind picking them up for us? We may get back in time, but the weather's not good and we were a little bit longer with Jack than I expected ."

"No problem. Where do you want me to take them?" asked Val.

"Take them to mine" shouted Sue from the driving seat. "You've got a key. Let yourself in and give them a drink or whatever. I'll sort tea out when we get back. We won't be too far behind you but we won't be panicking if we do get stuck in traffic" finished Sue.

"Ok. That's fine" said Val. "I'll see you back at yours in a little while.....and drive safely!" concluded Val.

Chapter 14

Val parked her car at Sue's and walked to the school to collect the children. She didn't want to collect them in the car as she hadn't got the appropriate seats for them all, and as it had stopped raining thought it wouldn't do them any harm to walk the short distance to Sue and Neil's house.

Val felt relieved that Jack was out of danger. She couldn't even begin to think about not having Rupert in her life. They both worked hard but they also played hard and enjoyed being with each other. She also loved the relationship she had with her two friends. They were all different but had solid friendships and enjoyed being with each other. Val also loved the children and enjoyed the 'family' gatherings they shared even though she had no children of her own.

She felt a bit better today after feeling really under the weather the day before. She couldn't put her finger on what it was. Both her and Rupert had eaten the same meals but she had felt really off yesterday afternoon.

It couldn't have been the cake in 'Mugs with Hugs'......

She was thinking about the conversation they had had yesterday about Alice and Brian. Val was quite shocked as she thought they were an absolutely solid couple. She just hoped that things sorted themselves out. She must remember to go to church on Sunday to help Sue sort out stalls for the Easter thing. She didn't go to church every week by any stretch of the imagination, but she did go and always went when Sue needed to 'round up the troops' as she put it.

As she approached the school gates a group of mothers caught her eye.....they were clearly having an in depth conversation. The nearer she got she could hear the names.....Alice and Brian! Oh dear, thought Val. Sue will not be happy about this!

After five minutes the children started coming out of their classes. She kept a close eye for her friend's children and saw Joe and Bobby crossing the playground. As she waved to them Maisie and Flora appeared and they all started running towards her.

As she met them at the gate they all wanted to know where their mums were. Val explained that they were delayed but would be home shortly and they were going to Sue's for tea.

Just as she was finishing explaining Adam arrived at the gate.

"Auntie Val.... What are you doing here? You don't usually pick us up from school."

"Your mum has got delayed from an errand with Auntie Delia so asked me to come and meet you. Hope that's ok?" queried Val.

"Absolutely fine by me" said Adam.

"Right, come on then gang. Bobby and Joe I want your hands..... Maisie and Flora walk just in front so that I can see you" instructed Val as Adam walked alongside.

It only took a few minutes to walk to Sue and Neil's house and they got in just before the rain started again.

"Right you lot....coats off, shoes off and I'll make some drinks" said Val as they did as asked and chatted away.

Once in the kitchen Adam told Val where all the drinks were and also where the biscuits were kept! Val made the drinks and as the children sat at the kitchen table munching

biscuits Sue and Delia arrived.

Val immediately put the kettle on.

After shouts of “where’ve you been mum?” and “what’s for tea?”..... Sue asked them if they would like another sleepover tonight.

Val noticed that Delia looked quite drained and gave her a cuppa as soon as the tea had brewed.

The children were all happy to have another sleepover, so Sue and Val took Delia into the little den to have their drinks.

Delia knew that she would have to talk to the children, so once they had finished their drinks Delia summoned Maisie and Joe into the den whilst Sue and Val kept Bobby, Flora and Adam occupied.

Sue could see that Adam was puzzled and when he asked her why Delia had taken Maisie and Joe into the den she told him that she would explain later.

Delia, Maisie and Joe came back into the kitchen after about half an hour and it was clear that they had all been crying. Sue looked at them and when Maisie looked up she ran to Sue for a hug as Joe did the same with Val.

Sue’s children looked puzzled and Adam demanded to know what was going on.

Sue explained to them that Uncle Jack had been in an accident the evening before and was in hospital....but would be ok, but that it would take a few weeks. She reassured them all that he would get better.

“So” said Sue “are you all hungry?” The response was to cheers of “absolutely...what are we having .... And when will it be ready?“

The three friends laughed at the collective response of the children.

“Val...are you going to stay?” asked Sue. “You’d be very welcome”.

"Well only if you're sure." replied Val. "Rupert rang this afternoon to say that he would be late home, so that won't be a problem. But he also asked how Jack was doing," looking at Delia who smiled sadly.

"I'll give him a ring in a little while.......now, what do you want me to do to help with food?" asked the two friends.

"I'll do a big pasta bake....that shouldn't take too long and it will fill us up. There's a lemon drizzle cake for afters that I made the other day....so, you two.... go and sit down."

Before they managed to protest Sue said very quietly so that the children didn't hear.

"Go and update Val on the lovely Betty and I'll join you as soon as tea is on the go."

Delia nodded and beckoned to Val to go in the den with her as the children were playing quite happily and would soon want to watch TV.

Once the food was underway, Sue joined her two friends with cups of tea . The children had scattered to their bedrooms to play and were unbelievably well behaved. Maisie and Joe were a little bit subdued and Sue thought that her children had picked up on it and were trying very hard to distract them by playing games upstairs.

"So..." said Sue as she joined the two friends. "What do you think of Betty's little drama this morning?" She asked Val.

Val took a sip of her tea and paused for a moment.... "I think she's rather lonely and must have been devastated when she heard about Jack. The problem is that she doesn't think before she speaks. If she had taken Diane's advice then she would have avoided a lot of upset. But I have no doubt that she will want to visit very soon."

The three friends all agreed and were chatting when Neil came in.

“Hello you three muskateers” he laughed. “What are you plotting now?” he said as he gave Sue a kiss on the head.

“Oh... This and that” said Sue smiling at her rather mucky looking husband.

“Are you going to see Jack tonight , Delia?” asked Neil.

“Well I wasn’t sure as it means leaving the children with you again” she replied.

“I’d be happy to drive you if you want to go, and perhaps I could put my nose round the door as well?” questioned Neil.

“I would like to see him” said Delia....”but I don’t like putting on you”.

“Look” said Sue “you’re staying here tonight anyway so it’s not a problem. Tea will be ready in about ten minutes and I can sort out the children.”

“Well only if you are sure” said Delia.

“Right...that’s settled then” said Neil. “I’ll go and have quick shower and once we’ve eaten we can make a move.”

With that Neil retreated to the shower and came down ten minutes later looking fresh and clean ready for his tea which Sue was just about to serve.

The children were seated and chatting away and Val went to help with the dishes as Delia sat down.

It didn’t take the children long to eat their food and demolish the lemon drizzle cake so that they could continue with a game they had been enjoying.

Delia told the children that she was going to see Jack and that they were to behave. They really wanted to go with her but she explained that they wouldn’t be let in at night! She told them that as soon as she could she would take them to see their dad.

With that Neil and Delia left for the hospital amid Sue and Val clearing away the dishes.

"As I was approaching school this afternoon" started Val "I overheard some of the mum's talking."

"Oh yes" replied Sue.

"You won't like it, but I'm going to tell you anyway" continued Val......

"Don't tell me" got in Sue "they were talking – or should I say gossiping about Alice and Brian."

You got it in one" said Val.

"You'd think that they had better things to do with their time....they really do annoy me!" said Sue.

"Have you heard anymore from Brian" asked Val. "I find it really hard to think that they have split up..... They always seemed so, so..... Solid.... If you know what I mean."

"Yes, I do know what you mean and it is rather puzzling....especially if she has gone off with Dennis the demon!" replied Sue.

"I'm keeping an open mind until I've had a chat with Brian.....but it must be difficult sometimes when you are in the spotlight quite a lot. I just hope that it sorts itself out."

"Do you want to help with bath time Val......it might be a bit wet" laughed Sue.

"I wouldn't miss it for the world" came Val's reply . And with that the two of them went in search of the children to get them bathed and in bed.

Apart from Adam who was quite capable of bathing himself, Flora, Maisie, Joe and Bobby were all bathed and ready for bed in half an hour. The tired children made no

argument about lights out, and Sue doubted that they would hear another peep out of them tonight.

Adam had taken himself for a bath as Sue and Val went down to the den.

"I'll go and make us drinks" said Sue "Go and put your feet up...you look jaded."

"Yes, I do feel rather tired" said Val.

Whilst Sue was in the kitchen making drinks she heard a phone ring and then Val

speaking so she assumed it was Rupert. As she took the drinks into the den she could hear that Val was quite heated in her conversation, which was very unusual if it was Rupert.

"It's time you realised what a wonderful daughter-in-law you have instead of constantly criticising her. Jack was badly injured yesterday and Delia is out of her mind with worry" said Val as she put the phone on loud speaker.

"Yes but he's my son" said Betty "and I want to see him... It's only right...."

"No it's not only right" interrupted Val her voice rising with indignation "Jack is Delia's HUSBAND and the father of her children. They must take priority and you have no right demanding anything of her at the moment. Now I suggest" said Val not giving Betty time to interrupt "that you give some thought to the way you have treated Delia and how might be the best way for you to HELP, not cause upset at a time like this. It is help that is needed NOT condemnation." Concluded Val.

The phone line went very quiet even though they could hear Betty breathing.

"I think on that note" Val said gently "I will say goodnight, but I would appreciate it if you considered what I've said, and no doubt we will see you soon. Take care."

And with that Val disconnected the call.

“Oh my, oh my” said Sue “how did that come about?”

“I heard a phone ring and realised it wasn’t mine but it was by the cushion where Delia had been sitting earlier. It must have slipped from her pocket when we were talking.

When I saw who was phoning I couldn't let it ring – I just had to say something after what Delia told me earlier about Betty’s phone call. Betty of course, thought that Delia had answered and started dictating to her again about how dare she speak to Diane and that she was coming down regardless of what she felt etc. etc. So basically I lost the plot and you heard the rest of it!”

“Oh dear, I hope it doesn’t make things worse for Delia” said Sue.

“Well I doubt it could be worse – she’s like a little witch the way she goes on. I wonder how Diane copes with her” replied Val. “Anyway, let’s wait and see.”

“If she looks for her phone she’ll panic” said Sue “I’ll ring Neil and he can tell her so that she won’t be alarmed.”

Sue rang Neil and he told Delia where her phone was. She had only just missed it but as she was with Neil it wasn’t a problem.

Val and Sue spent half an hour or so talking about the fair that Sue was organising at church before Easter – the ‘Eggstravaganza’ which made them both chuckle. Val promised to be there on Sunday to help galvanise people into helping with stalls and also to try and distract people from gossiping about Brian and Alice.

With that Val said she was really tired and decided to get home before Rupert so that she could have an early night. Sue promised to phone her the following day and update her of any changes with Jack. With that, Val gathered her things together, gave her friend a big hug, thanked her for tea and then went home.

Once Sue had checked on the children she poured herself a nice glass of wine and put the television on. Neil and Delia wouldn't be back for a while yet so she could watch a serial she had recorded that Neil wasn't bothered about.

When Delia and Neil returned some time later, Delia looked much better. She told Sue that Jack was being moved onto a ward tomorrow and that she could take the children in the afternoon.

"I do appreciate everything you've done fore me" said Delia taking a glass of wine from Sue.

"You are very welcome - you know that" said Neil.

"Well all the same – I don't know what I would have done without you..... Anyway, I'll take the children home after breakfast in the morning and get the house sorted out and put some things together for Jack before we visit in the afternoon" responded Delia.

"Do you want us to drive you?" asked Sue.

"No – I think I'll be fine and it will give me some time to prepare the children. Jack is so looking forward to seeing them" added Delia.

"Well give us a shout if you need anything doing" said Sue.

Chapter 15

A lovely, bright spring Sunday morning arrived after spending an uneventful Saturday where the children played in the garden, Neil did some odd jobs and Sue caught up on her washing and ironing.

Sue had put together her plan and list of items needed for the 'Easter Eggstravaganza' that she would be recruiting people to help with after this morning's service.

Once they had all had breakfast Sue gathered her things together to get to church early to do the jobs required of a Church Warden. Neil would follow in a little while with the children.

Sue hadn't spoken to Brian at this point – just the email that he had sent to her about Jack, so she didn't know what to expect when she saw him.

Once in church Sue set about sorting out the candles and the hymn books ready for the congregation arriving for the 10 O'clock service.

By 9.45am the church was very full – unusually full, and she still hadn't seen Brian. The lay reader June, had arrived and she was getting herself ready when Sue spotted Brian at the vestry door. He was 'gowned up' and chatting to one of the sidesmen seemingly ok.

Val had arrived at the same time as Neil and went to sit with him followed closely a few minutes later by Delia and the children, who gave her a huge hug and quickly told her that Jack was so much better the day before and glad to see the children.

With the choir lined up ready the organ began the first hymn "Glorious Things of Thee are Spoken" one of Sue's favourite's.

She suddenly heard ppparpp, pppparpp, ppparpp....... And when she looked up could see Freddie just in front of Neil and Val whose shoulders were shaking almost uncontrollably....... "Oh dear" thought Sue, stifling her own laughter..... It was farting Freddie...... Who would have said loudly enough to be heard "oops, pardon!"

By the end of the hymn Val had stopped shaking and managed to take control of her giggles!

Brian opened the service in his usual affable manner but Sue could see that he hadn't had a great deal of sleep – he looked tired with black rings under his eyes. Thankfully he wasn't preaching today – June the lay reader was doing it. June was a very good preacher but somehow Sue couldn't keep her concentration this morning. Looking around the church were several of the mums from school – brilliant – except that several of them were the ones she had overheard gossiping outside the gates on Thursday! Sue smiled to herself and thought that she would take advantage of them being there. She wrote a couple of quick notes – one for Val and one for Delia, and as the service came to its 'notices' spot Sue got up to talk about the Easter

Eggstravaganza that would take place in a few weeks. On her way back to her seat she slipped each of her friends the notes.

During the final hymn they both turned and winked at her and she knew that she'd got the help she needed. The three friends would create a 'pincer' movement in order to 'enlist' or 'recruit' the nosey mums from school. Sue couldn't help but smile to

herself.

Brian concluded with the final blessing and invited people to stay for refreshments in the meeting room.

Swift as you like Val & Delia moved from their seats to the outer doors determined to stop the nosey mums from leaving before they had 'volunteered' their help!

The lovely ladies and gents who organised the refreshments had moved to the

meeting room and Sue was stopping people and talking about the Easter Fair. As she looked up she saw that Val had already nobbled a couple of the mums who were

desperately trying to leave. With a little smile Sue went over and spoke to Gaynor and Vicki......"I'm so glad that you came this morning" said Sue sweetly " and I see that Val has recruited you to help with the fair...."

"Well...I'm not sure really...urmm, we might be doing things that day" volunteered Gaynor – the gossipy mum from the school gates.

"Nonsense" said Sue "you'd make brilliant helpers, wouldn't they Val?"

"Absolutely" agreed Val "we need someone for the 'Splat the Rat' game.... So easy to organise and the children love it!"

"Oh thanks so much" said Sue "I'll put you and Vicki down for that and I'll give you the details the week before.... But of course you'll be in church before then I'm sure... So you'll know all the details" concluded Sue as Gaynor and Vicki were spluttering excuses .

Sue could then see that Delia was engaged in conversation with three of the other mums....Lorna, Sheila and Judith.

As Sue approached she could hear Delia telling them about Jack's accident and they were making the appropriate soothing noises. In fairness the three mums that Delia was talking to were nowhere near as bad as Gaynor and Vicki and she felt that they sometimes just got 'caught up' in the school gate gossip.

"Hello ladies" said Sue as she approached them. "Isn't it dreadful about Jack" she added.

The three mums all agreed and sympathised and offered any help that might be needed especially collecting the children from school. Sue could see that Delia was quite touched by this.

"Now.... We need your help with the Easter Eggstravaganza.... Where can I put you down to help?" asked Sue.

"Well I wouldn't mind helping on the cake stall" volunteered Judith "and I can make some cakes as well."

"Brilliant – that would be great Judith, thanks so much" smiled Sue.

"Sue, I'm quite willing to help anywhere you need me" said Lorna and Sheila quickly agreed.

"That's wonderful.... Are you happy for me to let you know once I've sorted out the list?" asked Sue.

"That's fine" said Lorna. "Are you coming for a cup of tea she asked Delia, who was quite taken aback by their friendliness. When they were with Gaynor and Vicki they barely acknowledged her.

"Yes, lets... I expcct the children are in there devouring the biscuits" said Delia as they walked to the meeting room.

Sue was feeling rather pleased with herself as she had 'recruited' some more

helpers and a lot of the regular congregation always helped willingly, so she knew that things would come together. She still hadn't had a chance to speak to Brian and as she made her way to the vestry 'farting' Freddie stopped her.

"Now then young Sue" (he always called her young Sue, which made her smile) "just let me know how I can help with your Easter fairy thingy – you only have to ask".

"Thanks Freddie, I really appreciate that" replied Sue and made to move but Freddie put his hand on her arm and very quietly asked :

“What’s all this I hear about Brian and Alice.... I don’t like to approach Brian for fear of upsetting him. Do you know what’s going on?”

“No – I don’t know anything only what the gossip’s have spread, I have emailed him but with Delia’s husband having been in an accident I haven’t had a lot of time the last couple of days. I don’t think he looks good though .” replied Sue.

“Please let me know if there’s anything I can do to help – or if you find out what has happened – I’m very fond of Brian – he’s like another son to me...... And they seemed so happy .” said Freddie sadly.

“I will Freddie – if I get to know anything, I’ll let you know” said Sue as she made to go.

“Oh and Sue” called Freddie “if there’s anything I can do to help that lovely friend of yours... Delia is it? Just let me know” and Freddie walked towards the meeting room.

Sue paused for a moment and thought how kind he was. They all had a laugh now and then at the nickname he had been given ‘Farting Freddie’ , poor soul.... But he did fart quite loudly a lot of the time!

Sue made her way to the vestry and found Brian hanging his clerical robes on a hanger.

“Hello you” she said “how are you doing?”

Brian looked at her with anguished eyes. “I’m ok Sue..... It’s just a bit difficult at the moment and I expect the gossips of the parish are having a field day!” he said sadly.

“Well, I think that’s something we need to ignore.... And I’m not going to ask you anything. If you want to talk to me I’m here.... You know that, and so is Neil” replied Sue.

“Thanks Sue, I really appreciate that.” said Brian.

“Look....what are you doing for lunch?” asked Sue.

“Oh dear, I haven't really thought about food these last few days.... So not sure.. Why?” asked Brian.

“ Come over to us.....I’ve got a roast on the go and I always do too many vegetables, and if you’ve got a quiet afternoon you could watch the footie with Neil...... I think it’s your team playing his!” ventured Sue.

“Now that is very tempting Mrs . Newton” said Brian smiling.

“Well that’s a date then!” said Sue with certainty. “Come over for about 2pm – I think the footie starts at 3 ish, so we will have eaten by then, and Neil will be

delighted to have some company..... Especially as it’s your team and his playing” she said laughing.

“Now I’m going to have a cuppa in the meeting room before I tidy up – I think you should come and make your presence felt as well and it will stop the gossips!” said Sue smiling.

“Aye, aye captain” saluted Brian smiling “I’ll be down in a minute .“

Neil and the children left Sue having a quick cuppa with Val and Delia before Sue locked up. The three friends agreed that the ‘pincer’ movement they had organised earlier to get some of the mums recruited to help at the Easter Eggstravaganza had worked well and they all had a little laugh at the way Gaynor and Vicki had tried to wriggle out of being involved!

Val and Sue told Delia that she must ring them if she needed them, otherwise they would all speak the following day.

Sue went home and told Neil that she had invited Brian for lunch and to watch the footie with him. Neil’s response was that his team had better win then!

Brian arrived just before 2 and having taken off his ‘uniform’ dog collar looked more relaxed. He told them that he had no visiting to do and was grateful for the invitation.

Brian joined in the noisy family Sunday lunch and then stayed to watch the footie with Neil in the den. Thankfully Neil's team – Manchester United beat Brian's Leeds United 1-0 so after several beers and banter with Neil, Brian took himself home thanking both Sue and Neil profusely.

Chapter 16

When Delia got home from church the children went off to play while she sorted out their school uniforms from the ironing pile, ready for the following day. She was just about to start lunch for them all before they went to see Jack in hospital when the phone rang.

As she went to pick it up she saw that it was Betty – Jack's mother on the caller

display. It only took a few seconds for Delia to make the decision NOT to answer it. She just could not face another barrage of criticism at the moment and it would mean that she went to the hospital upset – and she didn't want Jack to see that. Delia let the phone ring while she went back to the kitchen to get lunch sorted out.

Once they'd all had their lunch Delia told the children that they were off to the hospital to see their Dad. By the time Delia had cleared the lunch things the children were eager to go. They had their coats and shoes on and were both clutching little cards and gifts that they had made.

Delia smiled at them fondly thinking how fortunate she was..........

The children chatted happily in the car on the journey to the hospital. The rain had stopped and Delia was admiring the daffodils that created a carpet of yellow on one side of the country lane whilst thinking how beautiful the array of snowdrops and crocuses were on the other side . Her concentration was interrupted by her mobile phone ringing. As it came through on the loudspeaker in the car she could see that it was Betty – again! She took a deep breath and decided to ignore it as they were only five minutes away from the hospital. Betty would just have to wait – she thought to herself! Thankfully, the children had been busy playing a game so hadn't noticed who the caller was as they would have wanted to speak to her..... She would deal with Betty later. Now the time was for Jack.

Jack had been moved to a ward with four beds in it. The children ran excitedly to their dad and Jack was obviously pleased to see them all. Delia saw immediately that he had more colour and looked more comfortable.

"Hello, you two" said Jack to the children as they ran to him. "I hope you're behaving yourself for your Mum?" he asked with the question in his voice.

"Of course we are daddy" answered Maisie. "Look we've brought you some presents" she added.

Jack winked at Delia as he opened their cards and little games they had made for him.

"Well thank you very much" said Jack trying to give them both a hug, but struggling a little. "Now... Have you two brought something to do so that I can have a chat with Mummy" he continued.

"Daddy I've brought some colouring to do" said Joe.

"And I've brought my book to read" added Maisie.

"Very good. Go and bring a couple of those little chairs to the end of the bed then you can lean on the table Joe to do your colouring" said Jack.

The children soon settled so that Jack could have a proper conversation with Delia.

"How are you feeling – really Jack?" asked Delia.

"Well... To be truthful I'm really sore all over. I am pumped up with pain killers which helps – but if I wake up in the early hours and it's wearing off... I know about it!"

answered Jack. "However, from what the doctors have told me, I've been very lucky ."

Delia's eyes filled with tears as she nodded.

"Hey, hey... You can stop that" Jack said quietly to his wife. "I'm here... and on the mend, even if it will take some time".

"Yes, I know – thank God you made it." replied Delia quietly. "I don't know what I would have done without Sue and Neil though... And Val and Rupert have been

brilliant" she added. "We actually stayed at Sue's until yesterday, then I thought we'd better get home and sort ourselves out – and the children needed their own things."

Jack nodded." Yes– we're very fortunate to have our friends. Neil told me when he popped in that I only had to ask and they would do whatever they could to help. I'm really just so glad that they are there for you and the children at the moment."

"Jack, do you feel like talking to the police? Sgt Brookes phoned me yesterday to ask if he could interview you tomorrow and asked if I would like to be with you." Delia told him.

"I can't honestly remember a lot about it – but I'll tell him everything I can remember if it will help." said Jack.

"I said that I would let him know later today. Shall I say about 2 O'clock tomorrow afternoon? That is visiting time and I can be here for then. If I'm delayed I'm sure that Sue will collect the children from school." suggested Delia.

"Ok. That sounds fine." agreed Jack. "Now..... Tell me about my mother....." asked Jack looking at Delia's shocked expression. "Come on..... I've spoken to Diane who told me that she's been up to her 'tricks' again!"

"Oh dear" sighed Delia. "She was pretty awful on the phone the other day demanding to come down etc. etc..... You know what she's like and I know that Diane also had words with her...... It's difficult Jack" said Delia quietly so that the children couldn't hear "but whenever she comes she is always so critical of everything I do. I don't think she realises that we both have jobs and the children......." Delia tailed off as she was starting to get upset.

"Now look" said Jack taking hold of Delia's hand" DO NOT let her do this to you. If she rings again just tell her that you will let her know WHEN it's convenient for her to come – not the other way round. I will not have her upsetting you and if I need to ring her and tell her then I will do! OK?"

Delia gently nodded her head, but knew that Jack's mother could be very difficult to deal with.

"Actually, Jack" said Delia "she phoned after I got back from church but I didn't answer the phone – I was trying to sort out lunch and I just couldn't take it before I came to see you..... and she tried ringing me on my mobile just as we were getting here - so I didn't answer that call either!"

Jack laughed out loud when Delia had finished telling him.

"Good – I understand she wants to visit but it will be when we're ready, and if she phones again just tell her that *I say* she has to wait!" said Jack as he gave Delia's hand a squeeze.

"Come on you two – tell me what you've been doing at school this week" Jack entreated his children.

For the next ten minutes or so Maisie and Joe regaled him with stories and antics of things that had happened at school during the week.

Delia could see that Jack was getting tired and she needed to get the children ready for school the following day, so she gathered up their bits and bobs and told them to give Jack a kiss and hug as it was time to go.

"I'll phone you later once I have the children settled in bed" Delia told Jack .

"Ok. We can have a proper talk later" said Jack as Delia kissed her husband.

"Behave for your Mum – you two" added Jack as the children waved to him from the ward door.

It was starting to go dark when Delia and the children got home from the hospital.

“Go and sort out your school things for tomorrow” she asked Maisie and Joe “and then you can watch television for a while before tea.

The children scampered off to put their little books in their school bags while Delia put their uniforms together and looked at the tea which she had left cooking in the oven. As she passed the telephone she realised that there had been a phone call as the light was flashing. Her heart sank as she picked it up to check the caller – Betty!

Betty had left a short message asking her to ring her back. Oh no, no, no thought Delia – not right now and with that put the phone back in it’s stand.

The children watched some television, had their tea and were bathed and in bed in record time giving Delia some time to catch her breath.

For the past two days she seemed to have been going round in a whirl and only just come back to earth.

As she wandered into the kitchen to make herself a drink she reflected on her friendship with Sue and Val. In many ways they were an unlikely threesome......but they had been friends for thirty years – it didn’t seem possible. She really didn’t know how she would have managed without them over the past few days particularly as her parents were on holiday in Spain and wouldn’t be home for another month. She knew that had she needed them they would have returned in a flash – but she didn’t want to spoil their holiday. Then she realised that she hadn’t told them about the accident and would have to ring them otherwise they would be upset when they got home. She couldn’t face doing that tonight as she needed some ’calm time’ as she liked to call it, and have a conversation with Jack. She would ring her parents tomorrow after Jack had given the police a statement – she would be able to give then a fuller picture then.

After making herself a ‘comfort’ drink of hot chocolate she phoned Jack.

"Hello darling" Jack answered "are the children settled".

"Yes.... They're fast asleep. I think the last two days have been draining for them as well...they have been really good I must say.....maybe we'll give them a little treat when you're better " Delia smiled into the phone.

"How are you after our visit....you looked really tired when we left." she added.

"Yes, I was rather tired and had a sleep before they brought the tea round " replied Jack . "So tell me...what's been going on the last few days" he asked.

"Well , I'm not sure really....just the usual.....Oh no.... I know what I must tell you....about Brian and Alice."

So for the next twenty minutes or so Delia told Jack about the gossip that had been rife and that Alice had not been in church that morning and that Brian looked rather bewildered.

"Well, I have to say that I am very shocked" was Jack's response. "I would never have thought they would break up – Brian adores her and I thought Alice felt the same about him.....you never can tell. That really is a shame.... I hope they can work things out ."

"Yes.... I think we all feel the same" said Delia.

After a few more minutes of general bits and pieces Delia could tell that Jack was getting tired, so after telling him that she would be there with Sgt Brookes the following day, she wished him a good night and ended the call.

Delia sat for a little while watching television and just as she had decided to run a bath and have an early night the phone rang. Without thinking she answered it only to realise too late that it was Betty . Delia's heart sank the moment she heard her voice.

"Delia... Hello this is Betty"

"Hello Betty" said Delia bracing herself for the onslaught.

"Delia..." said Betty quietly "I'm ringing to apologise to you for the way that I've been with you.... I thought about what your friend said to me the other day and I feel rather ashamed."

"I'm not sure" started Delia...

"No, please let me finish.... This is quite hard for me.....I know that Jack is your

husband and that you and the children must come first, but I really do miss him....and I was so worried when I knew he had been in an accident. Having lost his father not so long ago I didn't want to lose him too" said Betty clearly now crying.

"Oh Betty, you're not going to lose Jack .... But you must realise that our life is here in Willbury and you will always be welcome...... But to be truthful you have never made me feel good enough for your son and I've always felt that you wanted to drive a wedge between us. I love Jack and always have done and I know that Jack loves me.....but that doesn't mean he loves you any less. But unless you stop this constant criticism of me...and how we bring up the children, and how I clean my house you WILL become unwelcome, and that's not what any of us want." Delia told her.

Betty was very quiet at the end of the phone and Delia could hear her gently crying. Betty....when do you want to come and see Jack?" asked Delia.

"Well, when would it be convenient?" replied Betty. "I don't want to get in the way" she sniffed.

Delia smiled to herself . "Jack's going to be in hospital for a few weeks. If you want to come down for a few days you could help with the children – they'd like that." said Delia.

"Could I really?" asked Betty.

"Of course you could" sighed Delia. "The children would love to splash their Grandma with bath water" laughed Delia,

"How about if I came down later this week – would that be alright?" asked Betty.

"I'm sure it would – I'll get the spare room ready. Ring me tomorrow and let me know what you've decided." said Delia gently.

"Thank you Delia. I'll let you know tomorrow what I decide." replied Betty. "Goodnight dear".

"Goodnight Betty" said Delia feeling extremely shell shocked. "Oh Betty, thank you for the phone call."

Delia sat down with a thud. Had that conversation actually just taken place? She sat for several minutes in absolute shock before she decided to have the bath she had promised herself.

With taps running and lots of suds from the lovely bubble bath the children had bought her for 'Mother's Day' a thought struck her. Something Betty had said about a phone call with one of her friends ..... It must be either Sue or Val as they were the only friends that Betty knew. What on earth did Betty mean? But whatever it was Betty had obviously been giving her behaviour some thought.

She'd speak to Diane tomorrow and ask Sue and Val when she saw them.

Chapter 17

Monday morning dawned and the usual organising of the children...breakfast...school uniform was taking place in Sue & Neil's house as well as in Delia & Jack's. Sue had quite a lot to do today but wanted to be available if Delia needed her so she was trying to make a 'plan of action '!

She walked the children to school and as they went through the gate Delia joined her and watched her two join their friends.

"Sue" said Delia" Would you be able to pick the children up from school if I'm not back from the hospital. Sgt Brookes is interviewing Jack about the accident this afternoon and I'm not sure how long it will take" explained Delia.

"No problem at all – you know you only have to ask" replied Sue. "What are you doing before you go to the hospital?"

"Well, I really need to get into work to sort a few things out. They know the situation, but if I can get in and see what's happening about Jack's workload as well, it will put his mind at rest" replied Delia.

"Ok." said Sue "I need to do some work on Neil's accounts this morning so I will be in if anything crops up and you need me. If you're not back by tea time I'll feed the children all together so that you don't need to rush in the traffic."

"Sue, you are wonderful to me....thanks" replied Delia giving her friend a big hug.

"I'll see you later – drive carefully to the hospital" responded Sue as she started to walk home and Delia went to her car.

Once Delia got to work everyone she bumped into expressed their shock at Jack's accident and asked after him. Jack was well liked and took an interest in everyone in his team. Delia knew most of them, even though she didn't work with them closely.

She spoke to Jack's boss – Richard, and explained as much as she knew and told him that he would be off work for several weeks.

"Tell Jack that he mustn't worry about work, the most important thing is that he gets well" Richard told Delia. "However" he continued "I've been thinking about the best way to cover his work" Richard paused and looked directly at Delia... "How about you covering it Delia? You know as much about the company as Jack and he will be able to give you the information that you need."

Delia was so shocked she sat down.."Well I never expected that, Richard."

"The thing is Delia, I've been thinking for some time about a more senior position for you. You are very experienced, diligent and discreet which is very important to us as a company and our customers" continued Richard.

"Well I'm really not su......" started Delia as Richard put up a hand to stop her.

"Just hear me out Delia" asked Richard... "I know that you want to be there to take the children to and from school, and I respect that, but they won't be little for long and you may want more responsibility at that point – and of course it will come with a pay rise".

"This is all very hush, hush at the moment but there are going to be some big changes later in the year and I have Jack in mind for a senior promotion" voiced Richard "if you could do some of his work for the moment it would help while he's off and also mean that I don't have to spend time training someone to do his job - even for a short time" said Richard "what do you think?"

Delia was very quiet for a few moments before she said "How flexible would my hours be?"

"You mean you want to be there for the children? Yes, I understand that. Look, at the moment, and in the circumstances quite a bit could be done from home so that you could work around the children and also when Jack comes out of hospital" said Richard, who then added "Look Delia, you and Jack are two of the most capable and well qualified people in the company – and we WANT to keep you, so if there's a way to make it work, then let's find it."

Delia was quiet for a few minutes and Richard didn't interrupt her thoughts.

"I don't want to say no outright, but with everything that's going on I just need a little time to think about it, especially as I have to leave to get to the hospital shortly" said Delia "the police are coming to interview Jack this afternoon" she added.

"Delia, that's fine. I'm not expecting an answer right now – talk to Jack if you get chance this afternoon, but it would be helpful if you could give me an answer before the end of the week" said Richard.

"Ok Richard. Thank you, really, thank you, you've been so kind. I will give it some thought and definitely let you know by Friday. Now I really must go so that I'm at the hospital when the police get there" concluded Delia.

"Give Jack my best and tell him that I'll pop in to see him later in the week" said Richard "and I'll speak to you later in the week."

With that Delia drove to the hospital with an awful lot to think about on the drive there.

She got to the hospital shortly before Sgt Brookes and a colleague. The Sister on the ward had arranged for Jack to be in a room by himself so that they could have some privacy for the interview and was kind enough to get them all tea when the police arrived.

Seated around the bed Sgt Brooks asked "How are you doing Mr Harris?"

"Not bad, thanks" answered Jack. "I rather think I've had a lucky escape from what the doctor told me ."

"You could say that" replied Sgt Brookes. "The lad that came into you came off lightly by comparison......but he won't come off lightly in court! Anyway, can you tell me all that you remember of the accident, Mr. Harris."

Jack looked at the Sgt and his colleague who was taking down the statement.

"I don't remember much to be honest...... I was driving along Sheep Lane at about 35 mph – the speed limit is 40 there as you know, but it is a narrow lane and you need to know the roads as they are quite narrow. It had been raining a little, so I was taking extra care. I was just going round the bend after Shackleton's farm – do you know where I mean?" asked Jack.

"Yes, I know the one – very steep bend where the road is quite narrow?" commented Sgt Brookes.

"Yes that's right" said Jack "well the car came from nowhere......he was on the wrong side of the road so there was no way I could avoid him. I braked hard but he was going so fast he went straight into me....." said Jack who was now sweating profusely just thinking about what had happened. "I don't really remember much after that other than hearing sirens.......then the next thing, I woke up in here" concluded Jack.

Having heard what her husband had gone through, Delia was shaking and trying to control her tears whilst feeling unimaginable gratitude that he was still here.

"You know that my car has a dashcam in it Sgt Brookes" added Jack.

"No, I hadn't realised that – now that will be very helpful if we can get the footage from it" said Sgt Brookes.

"Where has my car been taken to.... do you know?" asked Jack.

"Yes I do" replied Sgt Brookes. "It's actually at the police compound so that it can be looked at....I'm afraid it's not a pretty sight at the moment...but I'm sure the insurance will sort all that out!"

Jack took a deep breath "Can I ask something Sgt Brookes?"

"Of course...what is it you want to know?" the Sergeant replied.

"This boy...youth that hit me....was it his car?" asked Jack.

"Oh no" said Sgt Brooks "it was a stolen vehicle...... To be honest the 'offender' is known to the police and we were looking for him in connection with another, very serious case".

"How serious?" asked Delia.

"Well I can't say a lot at the moment.....but do you recall the shooting in Willbury a couple of weeks ago?" Jack and Delia both nodded. "Well, he is wanted for questioning over that. You've probably heard that we have one suspect in custody – that was on the news - but he wasn't working alone and we have an eye witness which suggests it's the youth that hit you. He was trying to get away as the car had been reported stolen and he was picked up on police radar. We knew who we were looking for. But I'm truly sorry that you ended up in the middle of it."

"Is that all you need from me now Sgt. Brookes" asked Jack.

"Yes, thank you for your time – you may be required to be a witness in court, as this case will go to court, of that I have no doubt....but it won't be for a while. In the meantime Mr. Harris, I wish you a speedy recovery ."

As they took their leave Sgt Brookes shook hands with both Jack and Delia and the young constable with him did the same.

"Take care, both of you....we'll be touch" added Sgt Brookes as they left.

Chapter 18

Jack looked tired after the police officers left and Delia wondered whether she should go too.

"Do you want me to leave you to rest Jack?" asked Delia.

"No I do not!" he replied taking her hand. "Tell me what you've been doing and how the kids are."

Delia told Jack that everyone in work had sent their best wishes and hoped he had a speedy recovery. She then told him about her discussion with Richard and the job.

Jack gave her a little smile as she finished regaling him with the information.

"What are you smiling about Mr. Harris?" Delia said to her husband.

"Weeeelllll.......I knew that there were some big changes afoot. Richard had sort of hinted as much to me at the beginning of the year – but nothing had been confirmed. He indicated that there could be a promotion for me if everything went smoothly." Jack told her.

"So why didn't you tell me?" questioned Delia.

"Hmmm....I had been asked to keep it 'under my hat' until things were more definite, and I didn't want to build up any hopes as I know it will mean a pay rise." said Jack.

"I see" Said Delia, just a little bit miffed.

"But what do you think about me taking on your job in the short term?" Delia asked Jack.

"Quite frankly Delia, I don't think Richard could ask anyone better. You underestimate yourself.....I think you could do the job standing on your head once you got yourself organised." said Jack.

"But what about the children and me being there after school etc." asked Delia.

"Look........if Richard is prepared to give you some flexibility I think you should consider it – certainly until I'm up and running again. It will be much easier for me to take back the reigns if it's you doing the job." commented Jack.

"Hmm" said Delia "Its just knowing that the children will be OK. I must admit that I like a challenge....and this would be different from what I've been doing."

"I don't think you need to worry about the children........you know that Sue will always help out with collecting them from school if there was a problem" said Jack.

"Yes...I know that, but I don't want to 'put' on her because she is my friend." said Delia.

"Well, looking at the time" laughed Jack "I assume that she's picking them up from school today!"

"Oh gosh – I hadn't realised how late it was....and yes...she told me not to rush back that she would collect them and give them tea" said Delia.

"Look....." said Jack "have a word with her before you make any decisions - tell her what you've been offered and explain about the children. She can only say 'no' and I don't think that will happen."

"Ok" said Delia "I'll do that. I better get going though as the traffic will be building up and I don't want to leave them too long."

Delia gathered her things together and bent to give Jack a kiss.

"I'll ring you later on" said Jack "and you can tell me what Sue thinks about the job."

"Ok I'll do that, but the children might want to speak to you before they go to bed so I'll call you once they're in their PJ's " replied Delia. "Bye for now" and blew Jack a kiss from the door.

It was rather overcast when Delia reached the car park. She would be glad when the clocks went forward in a couple of week's time so that the nights were lighter. Delia could hear the children laughing as she rang the doorbell at Sue's which was quickly opened by Neil who had just got home from work.

"Hiya" shouted Sue from the kitchen "I'm just putting tea out – come and have some....it's shepherd's pie – there's plenty to go round!"

Delia smiled as she went into the kitchen knowing full well that Sue had deliberately made enough for all of them. Delia felt truly blessed to have such good friends in Sue and Neil.

As Delia joined them in the kitchen Sue asked " Well how is the wounded soldier today – any better?"

"Yes, he's not bad. He's given his statement to the police" said Delia.

"Oh right....how did that go?" asked Neil.

Without the children seeing her Delia mouthed that she would tell them later....she did not want the children knowing what the police had told her. Neil nodded understanding immediately.

There was lots of chatter at the table from the children about the Easter Eggstravaganza as Sue had told them that there would be an Easter egg hunt. The children all wanted to know where they would be put so that they could find them. This caused great hilarity as Neil came up with some awful suggestions like – under the grid....behind the gravestones....up in the trees..........

"Aw dad...you're just being silly now" said Adam, the eldest of Sue and Neil's children. Neil, Sue and Delia all laughed at Adam's disgust.

"I can't tell you where we're putting them" said Sue "or it would be unfair to everyone else.....but I'm sure you'll have fun! Now eat your tea."

When they had finished eating the children were told that they could have half an hour play time together before Delia took Maisie and Joe home. While the children went off to play Sue put the kettle on and with their drinks Neil and Sue asked Delia what she had found out about the accident.

Delia gave them a potted version of what Jack had said and also what they had learned from the police about the driver of the car that hit him.

"Well it sounds as if there is a lot more to come about the shooting in Willbury...and if he's stolen a car as well, it's not looking good for the lad" said Neil.

"Apparently, he is known to the police" said Delia "and they were looking for him when he careered into Jack. I'm just thankful that Jack is on the mend – even if it takes some time."

"Well you know that we're here if you need us Delia" said Neil "and now I'm going to have a shower and leave you two lovely ladies to have a chat without me around!" he laughed.

"I did need a word with you Sue with the children out of the way" said Delia.

"Oh yes...anything interesting?" asked Sue.

Delia told Sue about the proposition that Richard had made to her earlier that day and explained about her reluctance because of the children.

"Delia" said Sue "you know that I will always pick the children up for you.....I'm not going anywhere, and even when I do the odd bit of supply work it's in the children's school anyway!"

“I know Sue.....but I don’t want you to think I’m taking you for granted. You’ve been so good this last week with Jack and everything.............” replied Delia.

“Now look.....you are one of the most clever people I know....and Val would say the same. You always put us to shame at school” laughed Sue “this is an opportunity that doesn’t come your way every day, and as Jack said, it will be easier for him. Honestly, it’s fine. If you need them picking up you only have to ask .”

Delia gave Sue a hug....”I don’t know what I would do without you” said Delia “but I think it’s time I took my two terrors home so that they can call Jack before they go to bed .“

With that Delia gathered up all their belongings and the children, and they made their way home.

Once the children were bathed and ready for bed they gave Jack a call and had a ten minutes chat with him about school and what they had to do that week. Once the children were settled and asleep Delia rang Jack for a chat.

“Did you ask Sue about picking the children up?” asked Jack .

“Yes I did and she said that it wouldn’t be a problem “ replied Delia.

“I told you so” chided Jack “So are you going to take the job?”

“I’m going to think about it for a couple of days. I’m in work tomorrow so I don’t think I’ll get to see you tomorrow, but with everything that’s gone on I just want to let my head clear before I give Richard an answer.” said Delia.

“Well whatever you decide you have my support” said Jack . “Have you heard anything from my mother?”

"AAhhhh well........" said Delia and spent the next twenty minutes telling Jack about the phone conversation with his mother.

"The strange thing was that she said she had spoken to one of my friends...so that has to be either Sue or Val as they're the only ones she knows, and I forgot to ask Sue this morning!"

"Whatever has been said has certainly made her sit up and think" said Jack.

"When would you like her to visit?" Delia asked Jack .

"I don't mind" he responded "it has to be when you feel up to having her stay.....have a think about it and then ring her....or perhaps ring Diane first as she will have to chauffer her to the station!"

"I'll speak to Diane first and then arrange something" said Delia "and now it's time for you to get some rest....so goodnight and I will speak to you tomorrow."

"Night darling" responded Jack.

Chapter 19

As Sue walked the children to school Joyce caught her up.

“Hi Sue...have you heard any more about Brian and Alice” she asked.

“Hi Joyce” replied Sue “No...not a thing. I told him that we were here if he needed anything and I think he appreciated it....it’s a bit of a puzzle if Alice has gone.”

“He didn’t look himself at all on Sunday” said Joyce.

“No, he didn’t. But can you imagine if he hears some of these gossiping?” Sue indicated to Gaynor and Vicki who were talking by the railings. “He must be distraught” added Sue.

“Anyway, how did you get on recruiting people for the ‘Eggstravaganza’?” asked Joyce.

“Not bad actually” laughed Sue. “We managed to ‘arm wrestle’ Gaynor and Vicki into doing ‘Splat the Rat’!”

Joyce laughed out loud...”Well done.....you couldn’t have persuaded anyone better” and they both laughed.

“Actually Joyce, Judith, Lorna and Sheila all readily volunteered to help. Do you know, they were lovely when they weren't with Gaynor and Vicki” Sue told her. As if to prove the point Judith, Lorna and Sheila all walked up as Sue and Joyce met Delia at the gate.

Judith was the first to ask “How’s Jack doing Delia? We have been thinking of you .”

“He’s improving little by little, but it will take time” replied Delia.

“Well our offer stands” said Lorna “if you need any help at all we’re all here for you.”

“Thanks, I *really* appreciate that” said Delia and after quickly telling Sue that Val and Rupert had offered to visit Jack that evening so that she could have a break, and that Val would babysit the following evening so that she could visit in the evening, Delia dashed off to work so Sue didn't have chance to ask her if she had made a decision about the job.

"Sue...we don't mean to pry, but have you heard as to whether there is any truth in the rumours about Alice and Brian splitting up?" asked Sheila. "We're not gossiping ,

honestly...please don't link us with those two" she said indicating Gaynor and Vicki who were really giving someone a going over!

"We really are concerned about them both....we've always found Brian to be a gentle man and Alice was always so sweet......" Sheila added.

Sue took a deep breath.... "I honestly don't know anything at all. I spoke to him on Sunday and offered support if he needed it and that if he wanted to talk both Neil and I were here for him......he thanked us, but I don't think he's ready to say anything at the moment. We just need to pray that things will sort themselves out..... But while you're here I just want to thank you for volunteering to help with the Easter Eggstravaganza...it was lovely to see you in church on Sunday. I hope we'll see you again soon....." Sue added smiling.

"I think you will" said Lorna as they started to move from the gate....."We enjoyed chatting to people and they were so friendly......."

"Well that's a turn up for the books" said Joyce quietly as they walked away from school.

"Hmm" said Sue "It would be nice if they came regularly....but let's see what happens after Easter. See you later."

The next few days seemed to fly by and before they knew it Sue, Val and Delia were at their favourite 'Mugs with Hugs' having their weekly get together.

“So” said Val “How was Jack last night? He was in good spirits when we saw him a couple of days ago...though I think he was in more pain than he was letting on.”

“I think so too” said Delia. “It won’t be long before he’s wanting to come home...but the doctors have said that he has to take it slowly.”

“Have you heard from the lovely Betty?” asked Sue.

“Oh yes.......” replied Delia “I’ve been meaning to ask you about that .”

“About what?” asked Sue.

“Did one of you two speak to Betty last week?” asked Delia.

“Oops” said Val looking at Sue. “I’m sorry....I forgot....I should have told you.....”

“Told me what?” enquired Delia.

Sue looked at Val and said “Go on....tell her what happened......”

Val told the story of Delia’s phone ringing when she was at the hospital with Neil....when her phone had slipped out of her pocket at Sue’s and of Betty phoning her.

“I was really annoyed with the way she spoke to you....and always belittles you...so I’m sorry....I gave her a few home truths............Oh Delia, I’m really sorry, I didn’t mean to make matters worse.......”

Delia looked from Val to Sue without saying a word then she started to laugh.

Sue and Val looked at each other puzzled......

Touching Delia’s arm Sue said “are you alright......”

“I’m fine” laughed Delia “don’t look so worried Val.....you did me a real favour......she has actually apologised for the way she’s been with me!”

“WHAT ” said Val and Sue together.

“She’s apologised?” asked Val. Delia nodded her head whilst drinking a lovely hot chocolate. “Well that’s a turn up for the books....how do you feel about it?”

“She’s coming down on Saturday for a few days....so we’ll see how we go.” said Delia.

“I don’t think I will let her get away with being so rude or domineering from now on. I actually told her that she would be welcome as long as she didn’t start complaining about how I clean my house or bring up the children!” Delia added.

Both Val and Sue stopped drinking with the cup half way to their mouths. They couldn’t believe what Delia had just told them!

“I spoke to Diane on Monday and she said that her mother was quite subdued but she didn’t know what had gone on until I told her. Diane loves her Mum but she also knows how unpleasant she can be and she said that she had seen a change in her in just a few days. So Diane will take her to the station on Saturday....I’ll meet her there with the children and then we’ll take her to the hospital to see Jack ” concluded Delia. “Close your mouths you two” she said to Val and Sue “you’ll be catching flies” and laughed at them.

“Well I am absolutely AMAZED” said Val.

“And so am I” joined in Sue “but it is long overdue....let’s hope she keeps her

promise and behaves herself!”

Anyway.....have you made a decision about the job?” asked Sue.

“What’s this....what have I missed?“ asked Val..... So Delia explained about the

conversation with Richard.

"I'm sorry, Val...I just forgot to tell you last night....everything's been so hectic this week. But yes, I'm going to do it until Jack is back on his feet and then we'll see where things go. I have got some flexibility so I won't be missing our Thursday gatherings!" laughed Delia.

"I'm really pleased for you Delia" said Val "You deserve it..... And I know Sue will agree with me when I say that you really are the clever one amongst us!"

"That's just what I said" agreed Sue.

"I think we should all have another chocolate chip cookie to celebrate" said Delia "My treat".

"Not for me thanks" said Val "I'm still not 100% at the moment....I've not eaten much of late, so I won't push my luck."

"Go on then...." said Sue laughing "if you insist!"

As Delia went to the counter Sue looked at Val and asked "Are you Ok. You've been a bit under the weather for a couple of weeks."

"Yes...I'm ok...I've had a lot of work on and I just feel exhausted all the time. I think Rupert might be planning a holiday for our anniversary.....if he is I hope it's somewhere warm and sunny" laughed Val.

As Delia came back with the drinks and cookies Sue said "You still want me to babysit tonight so that you can go to the hospital?"

"Yes please, if you're ok with that? You know that Brian has offered to take me?" said Delia.

"Oh that's nice" said Val "when did he offer?"

"He rang last night just after you had gone home - he really wanted to see Jack, which is very kind. So I thought, well it does give me a break from driving so I said yes" explained Delia.

“I’ll come round as soon as I’ve fed the children” said Sue “then you’ll be ready when he picks you up.”

Sue and Delia spent the next half hour telling Val about Judith, Lorna and Sheila at school and how enthusiastic they were about the Easter Eggstravaganza. They discussed the possible stalls....had a laugh about poor Freddie and his ferocious farting...but also said how kind he was. He’d been round to Delia’s with a card for Jack and a box of goodies which included some very nice biscuits which Delia had hidden from the children otherwise they would never have got to the hospital.

The ‘Three Musketeers’ said they would catch up later and then went about their various itinerary for the afternoon.

Chapter 20

Sue left the children with Neil to be bathed and put to bed once they had eaten tea so that she could get round to Delia's for her to get to the hospital to see Jack .

As she was leaving Neil shouted "Sue.... Tell Delia that if she wants to stay at home tomorrow I'll go and see Jack after work..... it might just give her a break".

"Ok" shouted Sue back "I'll tell her ..... See you later, and don't let Adam stay up too late playing on the computer!" Sue smiled as she went through the door knowing full well that once Flora and Bobby were settled Neil would want to play with Adam. Men! She said to herself ....they never grow up and laughed at herself as she started the car engine.

It only took a few minutes to get to Delia's. They would often walk to each others houses but it was a dark and miserable night and she wasn't sure what time it would be when she was leaving, Sue thought it best to drive there.

Delia opened the door almost as soon as Sue rang the bell.

"Crikey Delia, I nearly fell through the door" laughed Sue taking her coat off as she walked into the hall.

"Sorry" replied Delia. "I've just put the phone back to charge...Jack phoned a little while ago to speak to the children before they went to bed and to ask me to take him a couple of books to read."

"How does he seem?" asked Sue.

"I'm not sure really....I think he's in more pain than he's letting on....I'll get a better idea when I see him" replied Delia. "Do you want a coffee before I sort the children out?"

"You go and get ready so that you can get off as soon as Brian comes.....it's a bit grim out there tonight and you don't want to be rushing. I'll sort the children out, you don't need to worry about that. Whilst you're getting ready and gathering those books for Jack, I'll put the kettle on and if you have time when you're ready we'll have a coffee before you go" said Sue ushering Delia upstairs to get sorted out.

The children had just finished their tea and were finishing off bits of homework. Sue could get the children bathed once Delia had gone to the hospital. The kettle had boiled twice by the time Delia was ready but she was in good time for Brian so Sue made them both a quick coffee.

"Neil says to tell you that if you would like a break tomorrow he will go and see Jack after work" said Sue as they sat to drink their coffees.

"Ooh , now there's a thought. I could nip in tomorrow afternoon if Neil's willing to go in the evening...It just breaks the day up if you have a visitor..... Can I decide later when we get back from the hospital?" asked Delia.

"Of course....you don't need to decide now" responded Sue as they both heard a car door slam.

"I think this is Brian" said Sue. "You get your coat and I'll open the door for him."

Sue opened the door to Brian and said to him "This is really kind of you Brian...Delia really appreciates it. She'll only be a minute, she's just getting her coat and speaking to the children....How are you?" she added quietly.

"I'm ok" replied Brian a little too brightly "I don't mind taking Delia....I intended visiting Jack anyway so it's fine....." he trailed off as Delia arrived ready to go.

"Thanks again Sue for babysitting....we'll see you later"added Delia as Sue closed the door to them.

Once in the car Brian and Delia chatted about general things...the weather...the news..and Delia told him about their 'pincer' movement to get some of the mums involved with the Easter Eggstravaganza to which he had a good laugh.

Delia desperately wanted to say something about Alice but knew that it would have been wrong to say anything.

"I do appreciate you driving me here and coming to see Jack" said Delia.

"No problem. I've always got on with Jack and he's always willing to give a helping hand when we've asked him" replied Brian. "I was pretty shocked, I can tell you, when Sue told me what had happened...... Dreadful business".

As they pulled into the hospital car park the rain eased off and meant that they could walk to the ward without getting drenched. The car park seemed particularly busy tonight and it took a few minutes to find a parking space.

As they got to Jack's ward Delia could see that it was very busy. Every patient had a visitor which she hadn't seen before, so she gathered up a chair from the corridor so that they could both sit at Jack's bedside – there was only one chair by his bed!

"Hello darling" said Delia as she bent to give Jack a kiss.

"Hello you..." responded Jack" Brian. What a lovely surprise."

"Hi Jack" said Brian reaching to shake Jack's hand. "How are you doing?"

"I'm not too bad, thanks" replied Jack "I don't think I could manage without the pain killers just yet though!"

"Did the doctor see you earlier?" asked Delia.

"Yes. He gave me the once over!" smiled Jack. "He said that I will probably start some sort of physio in a few days. I don't think I'll be home just yet however...but if I can get moving – even slowly, I might be home in a week or so."

"That's good" said Delia and Brian together.

“Have the police been in touch with you Delia?“ asked Jack.

“I’ve not heard anything since Sgt Brookes interviewed you” replied Delia “Why? Were you expecting me to hear something?”

“I wasn’t sure to be honest. He sort of indicated that he would let us know about the lad that came into me....I know he’s under arrest, but he was injured as well. I wondered if they had moved him to a prison hospital...... Not that it’s really anything to do with me....just curious I suppose!” concluded Jack .

“What exactly happened Jack ....if you don’t mind me asking” said Brian.

“No it’s fine” said Jack. For the next few minutes Jack told Brian what he had told the police.

“Like I said to the police...I can’t remember a lot as it happened so fast ” said Jack.

You say the police said that he was wanted for another crime?” asked Brian.

“Yes...apparently. A very serious one the sergeant said. He said that they had one person in custody and the guy that caused my crash was being pursued by police – he had stolen the car that he was in” added Jack.

“From what the police said the driver of the car that went into Jack could be involved with the shooting in Willington a couple of weeks ago – did you hear about it?” asked Delia.

“Oh yes, yes, I did hear about it.....” replied Brian rather hesitantly “A bad business by all accounts. I understand the chap that was shot is on a life support machine.......poor soul” he added.

Delia noticed that Brian had started to shake a little but didn’t want to say anything to him so changed the subject to Jack.

"Here are the books you wanted, Jack.... if you get through those by tomorrow" Delia laughed "You'll have to ring me for some more!"

"I'm not that quick a reader Delia and I'm hoping that I might get started on physio tomorrow so I may not get a lot of time to read" said Jack.

"Neil's offered to come tomorrow night so that I can stay with the children....what do you think?" asked Delia. "I might be able to slip in tomorrow afternoon" she added.

"That would be good. It means the children aren't too disrupted and it will give you a break as well....I'll be glad to see Neil....he can catch me up on the

football!" said Jack.

"I'll bring the children on Saturday when we've picked your mother up from the station" Delia added.

"Ah, it's sorted out then is it?" asked Jack.

"Well I hope so" replied Delia.

"What's all this about your mother?" asked Brian.

"Well she can be very difficult and has been with Delia for a long time to be honest Brian..... but after a few words from Val she seems to have had a change of attitude – at least I hope so for Delia's sake" said Jack taking hold of Delia's hand "If she doesn't 'behave' herself she'll be on the first train back!" And with that they all laughed.

"I managed to watch the match on Sunday with Neil..... Sue very kindly invited me to Sunday dinner.... It was my team and Neil's playing so it was good to have a bit of banter. They have the luxury of sky sports – not something that runs to a vicar's stipend" Brian added laughing .

The three of them talked about the hospital food, the weather and Sue's incredible energy at getting the Easter Eggstavaganza up and running for the next twenty minutes or so before visiting time came to an end.

“Let me know if there’s anything that I can do for you Jack” said Brian as he shook his hand and moved his chair back into the corridor. He waited there for Delia to allow the couple to have a couple of minutes to themselves.

Delia gave Jack a kiss and told him that she would try and pop in the following day but would ring him regardless and then went to find Brian who was talking to one of the nurses. As soon as Brian saw Delia he said his goodbye and they went back to the car park.

Everyone was moving at the same time in the car park.

“Oh dear” exclaimed Delia “I should have thought about the end of visiting time and getting out of the car park!”

“No worries” responded Brian “it shouldn’t take too long.”

They were both quiet whilst Brian negotiated his way out of the car park and onto the road home.

“I don’t think he’s looking too bad Delia” Brian told her “Have you seen an improvement?”

“Yes, there definitely is an improvement, but I don’t think he’s letting on just how much pain he’s still in. But if you had seen him just after the accident......well....” Delia had to gulp down the tears.... “I didn’t think he would survive at one point, but the doctors have been brilliant and I know it will take some time before he’s fully recovered, but at least he’s here .”

“I’ve put him on the prayer list and I must admit that he looked much better than I

expected“ answered Brian.

“So what do you know about the youth that hit him?” asked Brian.

“We don’t know anything really.....only what Sgt Brookes told us....we don’t even know his name .” said Delia.

“Whose car was he in?” asked Brian.

“No idea.....apparently it was stolen.” replied Delia.

“What sort of state is Jack’s car in?” queried Brian.

“I haven’t seen it, but I rather think it’s a write off. It is a company car thankfully and Jack’s boss has told us not to worry about it – the company will sort out all the insurance and a replacement car once he’s up and about and ready to drive again. If he hadn’t been in a car as big as his the situation could have been very different. It’s bad enough really.....it doesn’t bare thinking about.” said Delia rather wistfully.

“So you don’t know anything at all about the lad that hit him?” asked Brian.

“No – nothing at all....only what Jack told you earlier. Jack’s car has a dash cam which the police were going to go through so it will give a clear picture of exactly what happened. But Jack is a very careful driver and it seems that this lad was driving very fast....I think the police were pursuing him” added Delia.

Brian was quiet for the rest of the way home and Delia could feel herself nodding with the warmth of the car so when Brian pulled up and said “We’re back Delia” she found herself a little disorientated.

“Oh I’m so sorry Brian....I’m not very good company at the moment! Do you want to come in for a coffee or something?” Delia asked.

“No. no.... thanks for asking but I’ve got some things to do and I think you probably need an early night” laughed Brian.

“Well if you’re sure....Sue is here and I’m sure she will want a natter before she goes home” replied Delia.

“No.....honestly I must get going.....but thanks anyway .” said Brian.

“The thanks are all mine Brian....I really appreciate you taking me and seeing Jack”

Delia hesitated for a moment then asked "are you OK Brian?"

Brian looked at her and gave her a sad smile. "I'm fine....you go and have a natter with Sue and I'll see you on Sunday ." he asked.

"Ok. Yes....all being well, but we'll have Betty, Brian's mother in tow!" she said laughing "as long as she's behaving herself!"

They both laughed and Delia went into the house as Brian drove off.

Sue had heard the car pull up outside and had put the kettle on. She would have much preferred a glass of wine but as she was driving would settle for a cup of tea. Delia came into the kitchen as Sue was getting the mugs out of the cupboard.

"How was he tonight?" asked Sue.

"Good.....not quite so tired and he was pleased to see Brian. He said that it would be lovely to see Neil tomorrow night - they can talk about football!" Delia laughed as she told Sue.

Sue made the drinks and they went to sit in the lounge.

"I thought it was good of Brian to take you tonight" said Sue as Delia agreed with her. "How do you think he is?"

"I'm not sure Sue...he seems ok, but sad if you know what I mean. But...you might think this is a bit odd..."

"What's that?" asked Sue.

"Well...he was really curious about the lad that hit Jack's car.....I don't mean just general interest, it was more than that. He kept asking me things on the way back and truthfully I don't know the answers – but he asked me at least three times if I knew who the lad was." said Delia.

"That is a bit odd" said Sue.

“It was really Sue....actually I nodded off part way home so I couldn't be

interrogated any more!” said Delia having a little laugh.

They finished their drinks and Sue went to get her coat. As she got to the door Delia said “Do you think Brian might know the boy?”

“I don’t know, but I wouldn’t have thought so” replied Sue.

“Only I just remember I overheard a snippet of the conversation that he was having with a nurse on the corridor as I came from Jack......he was asking about the condition of the boy, but didn’t know his name and the nurse seemed unsure as to who he was talking about.” Delia told her.

“Hmmm....if I know Brian he was probably just concerned – even if he is a bad

un’!” said Sue as she went to her car.

“I’ll see you tomorrow – go and have an early night, you look bushed” Sue shouted as she got in her car.

“OK. Will do! Night” responded Delia and closed the door.

Chapter 21

Brian walked into the vicarage thinking about Jack and how much worse the situation could have been. They were a nice a family – in fact he knew that there were a lot of really good families here. There was so much that could be done . Sue and Neil were so reliable and kind...... He knew he would have to talk to them soon.

He felt lost as he wandered around the vicarage trying to make himself

concentrate on the ever growing list of things that he needed to do. It was too late to write his sermon now so he would make himself a drink and check his emails.

He really needed a whiskey but settled for a coffee!

Brian switched on his computer only to find a long list of emails waiting for him.

It was surprising how many were just total junk! The delete button cleared several in a matter of seconds then he scoured the others looking for one very specific one.

There was one from the Bishop's office to do with admin..... A couple from some work colleagues....one from Freddie....bless him.....he was checking up to see how he was.....then he found the one he was looking for.........

Once his heart rate had slowed down and he'd read the email for the third time he decided that he should get an early-ish night as he would have to start planning tomorrow – he couldn't put it off any longer.

Chapter 22

Neil only had a couple of small jobs in the village to do today before he started a run of bathrooms in some new builds the following week so he would be able to see Jack tonight without too much hassle.

He would pop home at lunch time and see how Sue was getting on as she usually did his accounts on a Friday.

He smiled to himself as he thought of Sue and her two friends. He had known them all from school days but it was always Sue who caught his eye. She was funny and kind as well as being attractive and he considered himself to be a very lucky man.

This business with Jack had really made him think. Jack was lucky to be alive. Neil knew that they all thought that and it had really made him start to think about his family and just how much they meant to him.

Then this business with Brian and Alice. That really had taken him by surprise – I don't think anyone could have predicted that . It was really odd!

It was a beautiful spring day - the daffodils were out along with the crocuses as he pulled up outside his first job. He sat and looked at them for a few minutes. Not something that Neil did . The accident with Jack had clearly affected him more than he realised. It felt good to be alive!

It didn't take Neil as long as he expected to do his first job so he decided to do a detour on his way home for lunch.

Sue was in the study doing his accounts when he walked in and shouted up to her.

"You're back early" answered Sue.

"Yes, the job didn't take as long as I figured, so I thought if we had an early lunch I could get this afternoon's job out of the way and have tea before I go to see Jack." replied Neil.

As Sue came down the stairs she was greeted with the most enormous bouquet of spring flowers.

“Where are these from?“ she asked Neil who was standing with a huge grin on his face.

“They’re from me for you – the most wonderful woman in the world, and I don’t tell you often enough” said Neil as he gave her a big kiss.

“Oh you big softy” said Sue “they are beautiful....thank you! Let’s have some lunch .“

Chapter 23

Val was working from home today. She often did on Fridays and it was fairly quiet at the moment. She had a lot of planning to do as they had some huge events coming up after Easter.

It was a good job she could work from home thought Val, as she dragged herself to the bathroom. She'd slept in again. She seemed to be exhausted all the time at the moment and felt constantly sick. She'd felt better yesterday when she met the girls so she didn't say anything, but she had started feeling unwell again later in the day.

Rupert was insistant that she call the doctor if she was no better today. He was clearly very worried as Val was always full of energy and it wasn't like her to be so pale , off her food and sickly.

Once she was up and showered Val didn't feel too bad and started making phone calls about the events that she was dealing with.

Mary, Val's cleaner had arrived about half an hour before and after a quick 'hello' left Val to her work.

When Val was in Mary automatically made a coffee for Val and herself part way through her jobs. When she took Val her coffee today she felt that she had to

comment on how pale Val looked.

"Val, are you ok? You're really pale. Are you coming down with something?"

"I've been feeling a bit under the weather for a couple of weeks or so....I'm sure it will pass....thanks for the coffee Mary ." answered Val.

Mary wasn't convinced as she saw Val almost heave when she smelt the coffee.

“Hmmm....” thought Mary as she went back to her jobs “I wonder!”

Chapter 24

Delia had arranged to see Richard after lunch and wanted to get the house sorted out before she did so that she was ready for Betty – Jack's mother, arriving tomorrow.

Once she got back from taking the children to school she cleaned the bathroom, wiped down the kitchen and vacuumed everywhere before she put clean bedding on the bed in the spare room where Betty would sleep.

Delia had put the washer on before she took the children to school so she managed to get everything outside to dry before she set off to see Richard. It was a beautiful day today she realised and all the more beautiful now that she knew Jack would make a full recovery. What a lot had happened in a week!

Having had a quick lunch, changed into a work suit Delia set off to see Richard.

Richard was waiting for Delia when she got there clearly eager to know what decision she had made about the job.

After some discussion about the ins and outs of how Delia agreed that she would do the job until Jack was back at work . Richard was delighted and said that they could look at the picture again once Jack was ready to be back at work.

Delia knew that they were lucky to have Richard as their 'boss' after some of the stories she had heard about some employers!

As Delia left, Richard gave her a hug and said that he would be in to see Jack the following week and he was delighted with her decision. What Delia didn't realise was just how relieved Richard was as he knew that Delia could well have been snapped up by his competitors who were head hunting some of his best employees!

Chapter 25

Saturday morning arrived with a blue sky and lots of sunshine. Delia was collecting Betty from the train station at 1.30pm and then they were going straight to the hospital to see Jack.

The children were playing and happy to be seeing their Daddy later. Delia smiled as she watched them putting drawings together and bits of presents for him. She just hoped that Betty was a 'reformed' character.

The morning passed quickly and after an early lunch Delia got the children ready to collect Betty. Just as the children were gathering their things together for Jack the phone rang. Thinking it might be Jack, Delia answered it immediately.

"Is that Mrs. Harris" said the voice which Delia recognised.

"Yes" she replied.

"It's Sgt Brookes , Mrs. Harris. I hope I'm not disturbing you?"

"No, it's fine Sgt Brookes. We're going out shortly to collect Jack's mother from the station before we go to see him. How can I help you?" replied Delia.

"We've retrieved the dash cam footage from Jack's car and it's very clear what happened from the footage. What we need is permission to use it in court" asked the Sgt.

"I'm sure it will be fine but I assume that you want me to check with Jack?" queried Delia.

"Yes please – if you don't mind? It's probably easier at the moment whilst he's still in hospital. Once he gets home would it be alright if I visit him again to go over his statement? There's no immediate rush as the lad is still in hospital but he is in custody and won't be going anywhere anytime soon!" added the Sgt.

"That's fine" Delia told him. "Sgt Brookes – can I ask you something?"

"Yes of course Mrs. Harris. What is it?" replied the Sgt .

"Who is the boy – lad that hit Jack? Is he local?" asked Delia.

"His name is Jason Chadwick. He's 23 and he's been arrested on a very serious charge as well as the dangerous driving charge where he hit your husband. I think you'll find that it will be in the news early next week as they will be in court very soon. He's actually part of gang that operates on the other side of Willbury. We think this Chadwick lad is the ring leader and we are almost delighted that he has now been incapacitated so that he can't get up to anything else. You name it, and he's involved with it! But hopefully this will be coming to an end before long. Anyway, keep that to yourself for now....as I say, it will be in the news next week. Give my best wishes to Jack and if you'll let me know when he's home I'll arrange a visit." concluded the Sgt.

"Thank you Sgt Brookes. I'll let you know when he's home. Bye bye." said Delia.

With that Delia ushered the children into the car not wanting to be late for Betty!

Chapter 26

Betty's train was a few minutes late so Delia and the children were waiting for her when she alighted the train.

"Grandma, Grandma" shouted Maisie and Joe together.

Betty pulled her suitcase along as the children ran to her and gave her a hug.

"Hello Delia" said Betty as she got close.

"Hello Betty. Did you have a good journey?" Asked Delia waiting for some acerbic reply!

"It was very nice" replied Betty. "It's such a beautiful day and it is nice to see things from the train that you wouldn't usually see " she added.

Delia was a little stunned as Betty usually arrived moaning about no leg room – someone constantly on their phone or talking too loudly!

"Oh that's good" said Delia trying not to register her shock! "Let me take your case and we'll get off to the hospital ."

"It's fine Delia, I can manage the case. Here, you take these, they are for you" chimed Betty giving Delia a lovely bunch of flowers.

"Oh" replied Delia, a little stunned. She could never remember Betty giving her

flowers before . Had she really had a change of heart or was there an ulterior motive wondered Delia. Instead she said "Thank you Betty, they're lovely. I'll put them in water as soon as we get home . Now we must make a move or Jack will wonder where we are ."

The hospital wasn't too far and Delia managed to get a parking spot without too much trouble. Betty had brought a couple of books for Jack and some sweets as well and some for the children.

The ward was fairly quiet when they went in. Delia could see that Betty was anxious as she looked for Jack who was sat up waving as he saw them arrive.

"Daddy, daddy, daddy" shouted Maisie and Joe as they ran to him and gave him a hug.

"I hope you two have been behaving yourselves" he said as he winked at Delia.

"Hello Mum" he said as he held out his hand to Betty.

"More to the point – how are you?" asked Betty clearly trying to hold back the tears.

"I'm ok. Getting a bit stronger every day" responded Jack. The physio is getting me up every day and she said that they may let me come home towards the end of next week-if I can manage the crutches" he added as an after thought.

For the next few minutes the children told him what they had done at school that week – gave him their pictures – and showed him their puzzle books that Grandma had given them.

"Can we do them now?" asked Maisie.

"Of course you can" said Jack. "Sit at the end of the bed and lean on the little table ."

Delia had brought them chairs from the corridor so that they could all sit with Jack.

"Can I give them the sweets I've brought?" Betty asked Delia in a whisper.

"Yes, of course – they have been very good ."

Maisie and Joe sat quietly colouring and doing puzzles in their new books and happily munched on the sweets that Grandma had brought them.

"It was nice of Brian to visit the other night" said Jack .

"Yes - I really appreciated him driving. It gave me a break ." added Delia.

"Who's Brian?" asked Betty.

"Its our vicar – you know him. He's been here a while now. You saw him last time you were here ." said Jack

"Oh yes. I remember. Very personable with that lovely wife ." said Betty as Delia and Jack exchanged a 'look' which Betty picked up on immediately and asked "Have I missed something?"

"Hmmm..." said Delia as she raised her eyebrows and nodded towards the children..

"I'll tell you later!"

Betty nodded realising that there was a story to be had.

"I had a phone call from Sgt Brookes just before I came out, Jack" Delia told her husband.

"Oh yes. What did he want?" replied Jack.

"They've retrieved the dash cam from your car and wanted permission to use it in court - I said that I was sure it would be OK but would check with you." said Delia.

"Absolutely" responded Jack .

"He would like to come and see you again once you're home" added Delia "and he asked me to let him know – if that's alright with you?"

"That's fine. There may be one or two things he needs to double check, but I would have thought that the dash cam made it clear." said Jack .

"I asked him about the lad that hit you" Delia told him "and he gave me his name, because he said it is going to be in the news next week. He is apparently wanted for another very serious offence and he has been arrested – even though he's still in hospital. He will be going straight to the cells when he's discharged."

"You know Delia" said Jack "Brian seemed very keen to know about what happened in the crash and about the driver, I thought ."

"You're quite right – on the way home he must have asked me about three times if I knew who the driver was! Actually I fell asleep" laughed Delia "but I didn't know anything anyway. I did think it was a little odd however and I told Sue when I got in."

"Perhaps he was just a bit curious" added Betty.

"Yes, maybe......" said Delia thoughtfully.

"Anyway, we had probably be getting back so that we don't get stuck in the car park" said Delia. "We'll come tomorrow afternoon."

Jack gave the children a hug and they gathered up their books. Betty gave Jack a hug and said she would see him the following afternoon and ushered the children into corridor to give Delia and Jack a minute together.

"Has she been OK?" asked Jack referring to his mother.

"Well she actually brought me a bunch of flowers" whispered Delia as she giggled!

"Wow – that's turn up for the books" laughed Jack .

"I'll see you tomorrow – but we'll ring you when the children are ready for bed so that they can say goodnight to you" said Delia and with that gave Jack a kiss .

As she walked towards the door Jack shouted "Don't forget to put your clocks forward tonight ."

"Oh I'd completely forgotten" said Delia "thanks for the reminder" and waved as she joined the children and Betty.

Chapter 27

It was a bright sunny Sunday and Betty agreed to join Delia and the children for the morning service. Delia knew that Val wouldn't be there as they had gone to see Rupert's parents that weekend so she would help Sue 'recruit' a few more to help at the Easter Eggstravaganza which was fast approaching.

As Delia was going into church she felt a tap on her shoulder.....

"Good morning.....how's Jack doing?"....... It was Lorna from school.

"Oh hello Lorna........it's nice to see you " responded Delia "Sue *will* be pleased that you've come" at which Lorna beamed her lovely smile. "Jack's doing quite well thanks. The physio is getting him up and there's a suggestion that he may be allowed home later this week.... Or early next week" Delia added as an after thought.

"I'm very pleased to hear that" replied Lorna just as she spotted Judith waving to her from a pew.

"I'll see you after the service" she added and made her way to join Judith.

As Delia got herself and Betty settled and the children ready for Sunday school Sue came up.

"Hello Betty...it's lovely to see you again.....how are you?" asked Sue.

"Hello Sue" replied Betty giving her a hug. "I'm fine thanks, and feel better now that I've seen Jack".

"Good" said Sue quickly aware that the service would be starting in a couple of minutes "I'll catch up with you properly after the service."

Brian led the service and looked a little better this morning – not quite as ashen as he had looked. There had definitely been an increase in numbers attending since all the fuss about Alice leaving but Sue hoped that the gossip would die down with the passing of time.

Sue made her usual appeal for help with the Easter Eggstravaganza after the service and she was pleased that several more people offered to help. All she could hope for now was some good weather. Now that she had a good group of people to help she could put the planning and advertising into place.

As she was making her way to join her friends for a drink in the meeting room she heard – before she saw him 'farting' Freddie approaching. Prrrp , prrp, prrp...oh, she thought, he sounded liked wet shoes squelching! As he caught up with her she turned.

"Ah, Sue. I wanted a quiet word with you" said Freddie.

"Hello Freddie. How are you?" asked Sue, always absolutely polite to this lovely generous man.

"I'm fine Sue. Thank you for asking" replied Freddie. "I was just wondering if Brian had said anything about Alice...... He doesn't seem to want to talk and I've always had such a good relationship with him. I'm rather concerned Sue."

"I know Freddie. He's said nothing to me either.....I think we just have to wait until he's ready to talk. But he did go and see Jack the other day.....so he is getting out and getting on with parish work. I know that he's arranged to go in school next week to do an assembly......so.....I think we have to be patient and be here for him when *he's* ready."

"Well you will let me know if you find anything out, and if there's anything I can do won't you Sue?" added Freddie .

"Of course I will....it goes without saying. Now come on, let's get a coffee and see who else I can persuade to help with the Easter Eggstravaganza" said Sue laughing.

Freddie immediately let out one of his belly laughs and said :

“Come on Sue, I’ll lend you a hand” as they both laughed and went to join their friends.

Chapter 28

The following week seemed to fly by and before they knew it Thursday had arrived and Sue, Val and Delia were in Mugs with Hugs for their weekly get together.

“So how are things going with Betty?” asked Val.

“Well actually Val , far better than I could have hoped for. She’s really been helpful. She’s been ironing and even cooked a couple of meals and told me not to worry if I’m late from work – she’ll pick the children up!” Delia told her.

Sue had ordered their drinks and added.... “Yes, I got quite a surprise to see her at the school gates and she was very friendly as well. Do you think the ‘penny has dropped’?“ added Sue.

“Well it flaming’ well should have” said Val before either of them could say another word.

“The way she has treated you Delia, has been disgraceful . She doesn’t know how lucky she is!”

Val was in full flow and Sue and Delia smiled at her, but they knew her feelings were only out of love and concern for their friend . Val saw their faces and smiled “Oh dear...on my soapbox?” and the three of them laughed.

“I’m going to see Jack this afternoon” said Delia “and there’s a possibility that they may let him come home tomorrow....or early next week, if not tomorrow .”

“That is good news” replied Val “how will you cope with Betty once Jack’s home?”

“To be honest, she’s been really good.....as long as she doesn’t take over she could be quite a help.....but having said that I’m sure that she will want to get back home soon anyway, so I don’t think it will be an issue. Interestingly Diane phoned last night and I managed a quiet word with her while Betty was reading a story to the children. Diane was pleased that she was 'behaving' as she put it, but if there was a problem she said to ring her and she would have a word with Betty ."

"I think your conversation Val, may well have made her realise that she had behaved very badly towards you Delia in the past, and that she needed to try and put things right ." said Sue wistfully .

They were all quiet for a moment while they savoured their drinks and cookies.

"Anyway..." said Sue "how was your weekend with Rupert's parents?"

Val laughed. "Oh you know...they adore Rupert and make such a fuss of me......it was lovely. They always go to such a lot of trouble, and they took us out for a meal on Saturday night........." Val stopped abruptly.

Sue and Delia looked at her. "And......" asked Sue.

Val looked at them both as her eyes filled with tears.

Alarmed both Delia and Sue took hold of Val's hands.

"Whatever is the matter?" asked Delia .

"Oh dear...I made a such a fool of myself" said Val as the tears trickled down her cheeks.

"I don't believe that" said Delia. "What happened?"

Val dried her tears and explained.

"We ordered our food and were chatting.....the starters came and we ate those – which were very nice....and then the main course came. That was fine. All of a sudden – without any explanation, I started to feel sick! I must have changed colour as Rupert looked at me and asked if I was ok. I could barely speak....and I had to dash to the loo....where I threw up just about everything that my stomach contained. I was soooooo embarrassed.......... A few minutes later Nina – Rupert's Mum came to find me. I have to say that she was lovely with me and insisted that we go home...which actually made me feel worse! I insisted that they finish their meals and I would wait in the ladies – it's a bit posh" Val laughed "rather like a boudoir with nice chairs and mirrors.....but to be honest I couldn't stand the smell of the food! Anyway, they obviously rushed their meal as Nina came back for me in record time. The hotel restaurant were very concerned that it was something they had served so wouldn't let them pay! Which was quite funny really. Anyway, I was fine on Sunday when I got up and have been since."

Sue and Delia looked at each other.

"Val" said Sue "I think you should see a doctor..... You've not been well for weeks now. It wouldn't hurt to get checked over ."

"I agree" said Delia. "Sue is right....you've been under the weather for a while and we've been worried about you. Please, Val.... Make an appointment to see your doctor...and don't leave it for weeks until you're sick again!"

Val looked thoughtful before she spoke. "OK. I must admit that Rupert said the same when we got home .....but I just thought it was something and nothing and had past.......but I was so embarrassed on Saturday! She said as she shook her head.

"You promise you'll make an appointment in the next couple of days?" asked Delia.

"Ok. I promise....if it'll put everyone's minds at rest " agreed Val.

"Now...I missed the going on at church on Sunday.....so come on....tell all...." Val laughed.

Sue updated both Val and Delia with the plans for the Easter Eggstravaganza which was now just over a week away.

"My main concern is the weather which I know we can't predict" said Sue "but if it's really bad weather – well rain really – it could literally be a 'wash out'!"

Val and Delia exchanged a look which Sue immediately picked up on.

"What was that look for?" demanded Sue. Val and Delia looked at each other

before Delia said "I think you should tell her Val ."

"Tell me WHAT exactly?" demanded Sue.

Val smiled. "It's ok Sue...we've got the weather covered."

"Got the weather 'covered'" imitated Sue. "How on earth can you have the weather 'covered'?"

"Sue.....do I, or do I not, work for one of the biggest corporate entertainment

companies ...and do I, or do I not have access to marquees?!"

"Yes, I know that" said Sue getting a bit shirty "but we can't afford to hire marquees – it would cost a fortune!"

"You're not going to hire them Sue....we're going to provide them" said Val. "It's all arranged. Rodney is more than happy to support the event – I didn't even need to twist his arm. He's always had a great deal of respect and admiration for what you do and the fact that you've got me involved he found very funny – so -if you want marquees – rain or no rain – they're yours! You only have to say the word."

"Well....I don't know what to say ...oh Val....thank you, thank you so much...that really takes a great weight off my mind." said Sue. "When do you need to know by?"

"I would need to organise the men to erect them...so by Wednesday of next week at the latest?" said Val.

“That’s absolutely great – I just need to get my head round it and look at the stalls and the weather forecast” laughed Sue “and then we can make a decision.

I am really grateful. There’s such a lot of planning goes into these events and the weather can spoil it in one fell swoop....so thank you – and thank Rodney for me.”

As they finished their drinks and gathered their things Delia said “Have you seen that they’ve released the name of the chap who shot the old man in Willbury a few weeks ago......it’s the same bloke who hit Jack in the car .”

“No” said Val sitting down again.

“Are you sure” asked Sue.

“Yes... The police had told us last week that they would be releasing his name this week as he has been charged with attempted murder – which if the man doesn’t pull through will become a murder charge along with the dangerous - or reckless driving charge. Apparently he is ‘known’ to the police and they have him linked to an organised crime group! It looks like he’ll be going away for a long time ” concluded Delia.

The three women were all silent for a few minutes whilst they gathered their thoughts.

“Right come on....onwards and upwards.....” said Sue “don’t forget to make a doctor’s appointment you” she said looking at Val who saluted her with an “ay, ay captain” and to Delia” let us know how you get on at the hospital when you see Jack later.

With that they gave each other a hug and agreed to speak later.

Chapter 29

When Sue got home she looked at the plans for the Easter Eggstravagnza. She was delighted that she managed to recruit so many people to help, especially as the other Church Warden was away in Australia visiting his daughter. Being quite new to the job she'd put on a bit of bravado when he asked her if she could manage on her own —and said "Oh yes, don't worry Derek I'll manage fine – you go and enjoy yourself!" That was over three months ago. Derek and his wife Jean had actually gone for Christmas.....but had stayed longer. They were due back over a month ago and showed no signs of returning, so Sue, along with a few others were quietly wondering whether they would actually come home.

Anyway, in the mean time Sue had got on with learning the job and working with Brian and other members of the PCC who had been only too willing to help her. In a way she had enjoyed finding her own way to do things. They probably wouldn't be Derek's way, but what did that matter really as long as everything ticked over. Which they had done until Alice went 'AWOL'!

Enough of that! She sat at the table with her lists and sheets and plans. Whilst she was doing her plan Neil arrived home.

"Hello you" Sue said as her husband wandered in to see what she was doing. "What are you doing home?"

"I've finished the job at that new house – it was quite straightforward as there's no one living there yet, so it was easy to get things done. Have you had lunch?" asked Neil.

"Is it that time...well no actually I haven't...I'll make something for both of us now." responded Sue.

"No. Don't do that. How about we have a drive to that little pub on the road to Welkley? We've not had chance to that for ages – just the two of us "smiled Neil.

“That would be lovely....are you going like that?” Laughed Sue looking at Neil in his messy overalls.

“Give me five minutes and I’ll look like a dashing prince!” shouted Neil as he bounded upstairs to get changed.

Ten minutes later Sue and Neil left the house for a quiet, child free lunch.

****

When Val got home from ‘Mugs with Hugs’ and being with her friends she felt thoroughly exhausted. This was not like her. Val was used to being on the go for hours on end and never flagged. When she woke up two hours later she was a little disorientated ......and got up with a shock when she saw the time. Then sat down quickly as she felt light headed. At that point Sue’s voice echoed in her head about getting a doctor’s appointment. She picked up the phone and dialled............

****

As Delia walked into the house she could hear the radio and Betty singing along. BETTY SINGING ALONG!! Good gracious what was going on! Betty had never been cheerful when she was with Delia. But....thought Delia....she had been incredibly

helpful since coming last weekend.

“Hello Betty” shouted Delia as she came down the hall.

“Oh hello love, I didn’t hear you come in” responded Betty.

Delia was a little bit stunned....I’m sure she just called me ‘love’ thought Delia......

“Do you want something to eat before you go to see Jack? You are going this afternoon aren’t you?” asked Betty.

“Yes I am.” said Delia. “Do you want to come with me?“ she asked as an after thought.

“Errm....no....you go and if you’re not back I’ll collect the children from school ” said Betty .

“Sue will always pick them up if we’re not back” suggested Delia.

“No. It’s ok. I’ll get your tea ready and the children can play if you’re a bit late back” replied Betty.

“Well only if you’re sure?” asked Delia.

“Absolutely” said Betty firmly. “Now...can I make you a sandwich before you go......?”

****

Sue and Neil got to the little pub - ’The Dirty Duck’ and were able to order fairly quickly. Sue told Neil about the offer of a marquee from Val’s company for the Easter Eggstravaganza.

“I think that’s a brilliant offer Sue. I think you should say yes, even though the weather look as if it could be ok. It would give us a bit more shelter and if the weather changed suddenly we wouldn't be worrying. I think you should ring Val tonight and take her up on the offer” said Neil.

“I must admit that my mind was going along that way.....I think the helpers would be less worried as well. OK. I’ll ring her later on” said Sue.

Both Sue and Neil enjoyed a lunch to themselves where they weren’t mithering about what the children would eat...what they were doing.....or where they were. Something that they couldn’t do very often!

****

Having eaten the sandwich that Betty had so willingly made her, Delia got to the hospital in record time. Unusually there was little traffic on the roads.

When she walked into the ward she could see Jack on crutches with the physio.

"My goodness....look at you" Delia exclaimed.

"Hello Mrs. Harris" said Fliss the physio. "If we can get him confident on these crutches we should be able to let him go home" she added.

"That's wonderful" said Delia. "When do you think that night be?"

"Possibly Monday, if he does as well tomorrow" said Fliss. "I've been checking with Jack about stairs and the bathroom etc. in your house. I think once he's confident on the crutches we'll be ok for him to recuperate at home, and to be honest, people get better quicker in their own homes" added Fliss. "Anyway Jack, I think that's enough for today. I'll leave you with your wife and I'll see you tomorrow. "Fliss helped Jack back to the chair by the side of the bed and took the crutches from him before saying cheerio to them both.

"She seems nice" said Delia.

"Yes...she is. She's very good, but she's a real task master!" exclaimed Jack laughing. "But I don't mind really as long as I get home soon......it's a bit wearing in here as it's noisy at night, they put the lights on early in the morning.....and you just don't sleep properly!"

"So you'll be glad to get home then?" said Delia smiling.

"That goes without saying" as he gave her a kiss. "Now tell me what's been going on".

For the next half an hour Delia told Jack about the police releasing the name of the man that had hit him.....about Val offering the marquees to Sue.....and about Betty singing when she got home.

"SINGING. Did you saying SINGING?" asked Jack incredulously.

Delia laughed. "Oh yes...she was singing. I was as taken aback as you are Jack. But you know" said Delia thoughtfully "She really seems to have changed . She made me a sandwich before I came out and called me 'love'!"

"No. No....you've got it wrong. That's not my mum.....what have you done with her? She's not been taken over by an alien, has she?" said Jack as they both laughed.

"Seriously Jack....she really seems to have changed. I just hope it's not an act until you get home.....we'll just have to see. But I'll tell you what" said Delia "I much prefer this Betty to the old one!"

****

Val phoned the doctor's surgery for an appointment which she managed to get for the following day. She had only just put the phone down when Sue rang her.

"Val...we'd like to take you up on the offer of the marquee for the Eggstravaganza. I really, really appreciate it. Even if the weather is good some shelter will be great to have." Sue told her.

"I'll get it organised tomorrow Sue...no problem at all. I'm looking forward to it and I'm sure we'll get loads of people there." said Val.

"Did you ring the doctor?" asked Sue tentatively.

"Yes Miss!" said Val laughing. "I'm sure that I'm just a bit run down...perhaps a bit anaemic."

"Best to be sure" said Sue. "Let me know how you get on."

And with that both hung up.

Chapter 30

The Easter Eggtravganza was the main focus for Sue the following day. She spoke to several of the mums at school who had offered to help, including Gaynor and Vicki who she had allocated 'Splat the Rat' to. They were more willing to help than a couple of weeks ago and she suspected that Judith had had words with them!

Once she got home she spread everything out on the kitchen table – the plan for the stalls – the remaining flyers- most of which had been delivered – and the timing for closing the village roads. She would phone the local 'bobby' when she was sorted and arrange it with them. The police were always very helpful with village events. It was a quiet village with little to worry the local constabulary so they usually joined in with village fetes.

Sue went through the check list : the posters and banners were up for miles around. The flyers were mostly delivered in the village and a housing estate a couple of miles away. They were in shops all the way to town, and there was an advert in the local paper. Sooooo..... thought Sue, "we just want some good weather and lots of people to turn up." She said to herself . She knew that she couldn't do any more and with that tidied everything into a file ready for Sunday.

Sue sat down with some lunch and her diary to check what they had planned over the next couple of weeks . Easter was only two weeks away which meant several services during Holy week. The children finished school the following week and her Mum and dad would come for the weekend of the Easter Eggstravaganza. The children had their usual activities the coming week before the Easter break, and Neil would have a few days off over Easter.

Sue's Mum and Dad didn't live too far away. They had moved from the village into a bungalow nearer the coast. It was about a forty minutes drive and they saw them regularly, but when there was an event on they liked to stay and Sue could always rely on their help. Her dad had taken early retirement from the accountancy firm he was a partner in. Sue reflected on how hard he had worked when she and her brother were small. He never expected to become a partner but it was the best thing he did as the firm was bought out and he not only got a nice lump sum but an increased pension.

Sue smiled at the recollection . Her dad was overjoyed at the offer that had been made and it meant that her Mum could also stop work. At the time her Mum helped with the dinners at the children's school, which she loved, as she saw her grandchildren every day. Sue knew that her Mum wasn't quite as willing to stop work as her Dad was, but she came round to the idea when it meant that they could have weekends away and holidays at the drop of a hat. Now – five years later, they both looked younger and fitter than ten years ago! She hadn't seen them for three weeks as they had been on a walking holiday in the Lake District, so Sue was keen to see them next week.

Her Dad also did the year end account for Neil which was a huge help!

Sunday morning arrived and thankfully, thought Sue, there was a good congregation. This meant that she could give out all the details for the Easter Eggstravaganza the following Saturday without having to chase people. Whilst she talking to some of the helpers in the meeting room over a cup of tea she became aware of Freddie – the usual Prrrp, Prrp, prrp, preceded him . Sue smiled to herself. He really must do something about his farting!

"Good morning Sue" Freddie approached.

"Hello Freddie. How are you this morning?" Sue asked.

"Just to let you know that I've got the champagne for the afternoon tea, and there's a bottle for the raffle." Freddie told her.

Sue touched his arm. "Freddie, what would we do without you. Thank you. You are so generous."

"Oh it's nothing Sue. Glad to do my bit. I'll be there to help wherever you want me on Saturday. Just let me know." Freddie reminded her. Then very quietly he said, "Is Brian alright this morning? He looks a bit grey and he's still not said a word about Alice ."

Sue moved him away from where people were talking so that they couldn't be overheard.

"I haven't really spoken to him this morning" said Sue "I've been trying to make sure everything was in place for Saturday as this is our big fund raiser.....I'll try and get a word with him before I go home and I'll ring you later" concluded Sue just as Brian came into the meeting room. As she glanced at him she did think he looked a bit grey and he definitely hadn't been sleeping. Before she could say anything Neil started a conversation with Brian......"I see your team lost again yesterday Brian" laughed Neil.

"Oh yes...they're not doing so well are they" smiled Brian, but the smile didn't reach his eyes and he definitely looked worried thought Sue. As Sue was thinking that she would try to speak to Brian during the week Delia came and gave her a hug.

"Hi Sue. You are so organised. I think it's going to be brilliant on Saturday and.......Jack's coming home on Monday" said Delia with delight.

"That's fabulous news!" said Sue giving her friend a hug. "I should think you'll be pleased to see Jack home, won't you Betty?"

Betty had been stood close to Delia having a cup of tea but looked rather sad when Sue spoke to her.

"I'm pleased he's coming home......" replied Betty slowly.

“I feel a ‘but’ coming on” said Sue . Delia had gone to speak to one of the other Mum’s from school so Betty was on her own with Sue.

“What’s the matter Betty?“ asked Sue who could see that she had tears in her eyes.

“Well.....I expect that they’ll want me to go home once he’s back” said Betty trying not to cry.

“Oh dear. I’m sure that’s not the case....anyway, I’m expecting you to help next Saturday at the fair!” said Sue.

“Really” said Betty “You want me to help?”

“Of course I do! Look I’ll have a word with Delia ....” said Sue.

“You’ll have a word with me about what?” asked Delia who had actually overheard quite a lot of the conversation.

“Betty thinks that you’ll want her to go home as soon as Jack’s home, and I’ve told her that I need her help next Saturday” Sue winked at Delia from behind Betty.

“Of course I want you to go home” said Delia firmly, then smiled her lovely warm smile.

“But not yet Betty if you want to stay” as Delia gave her mother-in-law a hug. By this time Betty was crying.

Sue moved away to let the two women have a moment together. This had been a long time coming for Delia, but Sue was convinced that Betty had changed and things would be so different from now on. In the end it was agreed that Betty would stay for Easter before going home.

Chapter 31

Jack came home the following day with crutches and instructions galore of what to and not to do! He was just glad to be home. Delia had taken the day off work to collect him and get him settled before the children came home from school. Betty collected the children from school and told Sue that Jack was home. Sue told her that Neil would call round later to see if he could help Jack in any way but that she must phone if anything occurred beforehand.

When Neil got home Sue told him that Jack was home and that she had told Betty that he would go and check on Jack after tea. They didn't know if Jack would need any help with getting around and Neil might be able to help. Neil willingly obliged once the children were settled and sneaked a couple of beers with him!

As Neil went out the phone rang only for Sue to find Val on the other end.

"Hello chief organiser" said Val in a very bright cheerful voice.

"Hello you" laughed Sue back at her.

"I thought that I would let you know that I've organised a couple of marquee's for Saturday and Rodney has done quite a bit of advertising amongst his friends at the golf club – so you might just get some hoy polloy there" laughed Val.

"That's fab Val. Thank you so much . I do seem to have recruited quite a bit of help and we've got lots of stalls. I don't think there's anything else I can do – just the 'egg hunt', which really can't be done until Friday night. Do you think Rupert might come and help Neil with it?" asked Sue.

"Oh yes – absolutely! Two big kids together there. I'll come with him and help you while they are hiding eggs, but I'll see you on Thursday as usual?" asked Val.

"Yes and yes. That's a good idea. Did you know that Jack has come home today? Neil's just gone round to see if there's anything he can do to help." Sue told Val.

"I wasn't sure though Delia thought he might come home today. It'll be a bit easier for her with him at home. Travelling to the hospital almost every day gets quite tiring" responded Val.

"You know that Betty's going to stay until Easter?" added Sue.

"EASTER!" exclaimed Val....... So Sue told her the story.

****

As the week progressed the weather got better. For April it was positively warm and Sue just hoped it would last until Saturday. Val, Sue and Delia met as usual for their Thursday gathering at 'Mugs with Hugs' and Val told Sue that the marquees would be put up the following evening and that she and Rupert would come early evening to 'supervise'!

Friday dawned with a lovely blue sky and Sue prayed that the following day would be the same. As she got the children ready for school Neil told her that he would finish early so that he could help her get organised for the Eggstravaganza.

"So what time do you think you'll be back?" asked Sue as Neil was about to leave.

"Hopefully between 12 and 1...can we have lunch then?" replied Neil.

"That's fine...that fits perfectly with me. I'll see you later" said Sue.

Sue gathered the children together and walked them to school where quite a few Mums were talking.

"All sorted for tomorrow Sue?" shouted Judith as Sue approached.

"Hopefully....I want the weather to be like this" laughed Sue.

"Well if you need any help today give me a shout" said Judith and one or two others nodded their heads.

Sue was delighted that so many had agreed to help. It had taken a long time to get the Mums involved – even though it was a 'church' school. If everyone enjoyed themselves tomorrow she hoped that not only would some of the newcomers continue to attend church, but they might get involved with events she thought as she walked home.

Good as his word Neil was home by 12.30 and whilst they had lunch they organised what they needed to do before they collected the children from school at the end of the day.

Neil had organised a 'map' round the village so that they could mark where he and Rupert put the plastic eggs later on. The plan was that they would hide or hang plastic eggs of different sizes around the village for the children to find and mark on a map where they found them. They would all end up with a chocolate egg, of course, but it was a fun activity for the children to do and it helped to keep them focussed for a little while. They had planned quite a few games for the children as well as some super stalls for the adults.

Sue had phoned Val to say that if they wanted to come early it would be a chippy tea before the hiding of the eggs took place. Sue also had to get three very excited children to bed. Adam was desperate to help hide the eggs – but largely so he would know where they were the following day!

Rupert had finished work early – even he was caught up in the excitement of tomorrow, so he and Val arrived soon after the children got home from school.

Neil and Rupert went to the chip shop whilst Sue and Val set the table and the children talked the hind legs off Auntie Val.....which Sue noticed she absolutely loved!

Tea over, the children bathed and the younger two in bed and Adam desperate to play with Auntie Val, Neil and Rupert gathered the huge bag of plastic eggs that Sue had organised for the hunt. Sue left Val absorbed in a computer game with Adam and headed out with the men as Val had promised to get Adam to bed in half an hour, so Sue went off to photocopy the map for the children to use for the egg hunt. Neil would mark on his map where the eggs were so that when the children finished he could check them off. The ones who found them all would go into a draw to win a large egg...so the children were keen to find them all.

When Sue got back home about forty five minutes later Val was tucking Adam up in bed.

"Do you fancy a glass of wine Val?" asked Sue.

"Ermm ....no I think I'd prefer a cuppa" responded Val.

"Friday night and no glass of wine – that's not like you" laughed Sue.

Val was quiet and didn't reply.

"You ok? Val . You're very quiet" asked Sue.

"Oh I don't know what's the matter with me Sue. I've felt really 'out of sorts' for ages. I went to the doctor and he's done some blood tests. Hopefully I'll get the results next week..........I just hope it's something and nothing" said Val.

Sue could see that Val was a bit troubled so decided to change the subject.

“I think Delia’s parents are coming home from Spain next week...they decided to cut the holiday short now that Jack’s out of hospital” said Sue.

“Yes...Delia said that they wanted to come home but she told them not to as there was nothing they could do.....they have been away for about nine weeks though!” laughed Val.

“Anyway, I’ve been thinking Sue. How about you all come round to us on Easter Monday? We’ve not had a good gathering for ages and Rups and I would like to do an egg hunt for the children – he really enjoyed the one we did a couple of years ago.... I think he’s just a big kid at heart!” said Val laughing.

“That would be lovely and the children would be thrilled....you must let us know what to bring....have you mentioned it to Delia?” asked Sue.

“No, not yet. I was hoping to get to chat to her tomorrow.” said Val.

“The only snag is that I think my parents may be here and I definitely think Betty will be” added Sue.

“That’s OK” said Val. “Let’s have everyone round....and you don’t need to do anything...we’ve already decided that we’re going to get caterers in” said Val.

“No, no...you don’t need to do that...we can all bring something” replied Sue.

“No! It’s been decided....we’re putting on the spread....it’s also our wedding anniversary that week....sooooo an excuse for a celebration” said Val.

“Of course...is it five years this time? How time flies!” giggled Sue.

Val laughed and they talked about Jack and the chap that was arrested....and how Brian was coping....or not....and the Eggstravaganza the following day.

Neil and Rupert came back about two hours later laughing as they walked in.

“They’ll never find all of them” laughed Rupert “you won’t believe where we’ve put some of the eggs!”

Both Neil and Rupert were laughing .

“You sound absolutely wicked” said Val which made them laugh even more.

“Well are you going to tell us where they are?” asked Sue.

“Definitely not!” exclaimed Neil “You’ll have to find them yourselves tomorrow”.

And with that they both collapsed in a heap of laughter!

Chapter 32

Sue was awake bright and early, thankfully to a beautiful sunny day. She needed to ensure that all the stallholders knew where their stalls were and that they had everything they needed. The police would block the roads into the village before 10am so that people could park in one of the fields and there wouldn't be any congestion. It made it much safer for the villagers and especially the children. There were three points of entry into the village and each one would be 'manned' to collect an entrance fee.

Neil was up and making breakfast when Sue went into the kitchen after her shower and the children were already eating. Sue smiled to herself as they were clearly very excited!

"Right mrs organiser" said Neil laughing "you need a good breakfast this morning as you're going to have a busy day......so eat!"

"Aye aye captain" replied Sue joining in the fun as she sat down to eat a cooked breakfast.

Sue considered how lucky she was to have Neil fully involved with this event not to mention all the other things he helped her with both at church and the children's school.

"Do you think Gaynor & Vicki will turn up to do 'Splat the Rat'" asked Sue.

"I don't know....did they say that they would?" replied Neil.

"Well we sort of bamboozled them and they said they would....I just hope they don't let us down" said Sue.

"What will you do if they don't turn up....have you got a back up plan?" asked Neil.

"Yes, I think so.....My dad said he would help if needed and he loves that sort of thing..but I'll have to ring him to get him here a bit earlier......I'll give Gaynor and Vicki the benefit of the doubt first and if they've not arrived when everything else is set up then I'll call in the cavalry!" sais Sue.

Neil made a noise pretending to be a bugler.

"Dad, what are you doing?" asked Adam.

"I'm pretending to play the trumpet" said Neil "why....don't you think I'm any good!"

"No we don't" piped up all three children together. To which Neil feigned mock upset and Sue laughed.

Sue finished her breakfast and agreed that Adam could go with her to help check the stalls and Neil would bring Flora and Bobby in a little while. Once Sue's parent's had arrived Flora and Bobby would stay with them to let Sue and Neil help wherever they were needed. Adam had agreed to help on one of the games with his friend Steven and his dad, so he would be occupied for most of the day.

Once the games and stalls were finished there was going to be a hog roast which 'farting' Freddie had organised, so she would be able to get a sit down at the end of the day.

"OK Adam are you ready, we should get up to the marquee before all the stall holders" Sue said.

I'm coming Mum...just putting my shoes on" replied Adam.

Sue could hardly believe that her first born who only weighed 6lbs when he was born would be going to high school in September and that he was as tall as her with bigger feet! The thought made her both smile and fill her with dread in equal measure.

Sue and Adam walked the few minutes to church and the centre of the village where the marquees had been put up the day before. Tables were being laid out with a variety of goods from beautiful crafts made by many of the ladies from church along with a stall of wooden items that one of the villagers made and donated every year.

After serious discussion with the ladies who did the catering, they had decided to have a 'Tea Room' in one of the marquees with waitress service. Joyce had persuaded her daughter and a couple of school friends to be waitresses for the day.

There was bunting flying across the marquees, across the green and outside the local pub who had made a very generous donation of a 'Barrel of Booze' to be raffled.

Sue stood and watched everyone beavering away and was quite overcome at the tremendous support she had received for this event. She didn't think anyone had refused to help and as she looked down the road saw Gaynor and Vicki walking up. Now that was success she decided!

Sue smiled and waved to the two women now making their way towards her.

"Good morning you two...it's lovely to see you" Sue told them.

"You're alright" said Vicki "Where are we then?"

"Come on ...I'll show you" replied Sue.

"I must say Sue, this does look amazing......" said Gaynor waving her hand around the village green. "And I think we may be lucky with the weather....it's already quite warm ."

"I think we've been very lucky this month" responded Sue as they walked over to the games area.

There was a table all ready for the 'Rat' and Sue went to get the prizes whilst the two women set it up.

By the time Sue got back they were already trying it out and laughing every time they missed!

"Oh Sue...this is going to be so much fun!" said Vicki.

Sue smiled.."Here you are... A bucket full of prizes for anyone who actually does splat the rat" and laughed.

"Billy will come and give you some float before we get going, and he'll collect the 'takings' from you at the end......" said Sue. "I must say, both of you...I'm really pleased that you've come...thank you ." And with that Sue gave them both a hug and to their credit both Vicki and Gaynor looked a little 'sheepish'. Sue smiled as she walked away knowing that they nearly didn't come. Very quietly Sue said a little "Thank you God" as she went over to see how they were getting on in the marquee.

During the next hour Sue spoke to every stall holder.... Directed people to stalls... helped the ladies display the cakes......set out the cups in the hall......spoke to the local police constable who would put the barriers up......and try to have a sneaky look at where Neil and Rupert had hidden the eggs ....without success!

When Brian arrived she gave him a folder with a layout of the village and church for people to place where the eggs were. Brian would work round all the stalls but was going to start with the egg hunt as he would see most of the children and he could chat to them.

Everyone now seemed to be in place....the barriers were up and she could see people waiting to come in.....so she shouted to the stall holders..... "Are we ready" and her answer was a huge cheer from everyone.

Within minutes the village seemed to be flooded with people. She was so grateful that the weather was good and that the advertising had been successful.

As Sue listened to the laughter from the adults and squeals of delight from the children winning goldfish she saw Betty pushing Jack in a wheelchair along with Val chatting away. Delia was already helping Billy with money and checking that the stallholders had enough change.

As they approached Sue smiled and said "Jack...how are you doing...it's great to see you here ."

"I'm very pleased to be here Sue....at least I can get a proper night's sleep at home.....it wasn't particularly restful in hospital" commented Jack.

"Hi Betty.....how are you? Can you manage that wheelchair?" asked Sue.

"Oooh I'm fine love.....especially now that Jack's home and in one piece" smiled Betty.

"This is amazing Sue" she added.

"Yes and we have to thank Val for a lot of this" she said smiling at her friend.

"It was nothing Sue....you're the one who's done all the hard work organising this and getting the donations..........I've just seen the barrel of booze from the 'Chalk & Cheese'....they have been generous" added Val.

"Yes, they certainly have....I've been quite overwhelmed at the generosity....not to mention Freddie and the hog roast later on ......it will make a lovely evening if the weather stays calm ." replied Sue.

"I'm just going to push Jack into the marquee for a look round girls....we'll see you later" said Betty.

As they walked away Val looked at Sue and said...." they were just coming up the road as I parked....I was dreading seeing Betty after what I said to her on the phone.....anyway, one of the dad's that Jack knew came to speak to him and Betty turned to me and thanked me for what I had said ."

"Never" said Sue.

"Honestly...you could have knocked me down with a feather! She said that I had made her think about her behaviour and she felt ashamed . She said she hadn't realised how cruel she had been to Delia and that she would do everything in her power to make it up to her....." concluded Val.

I am absolutely stunned" said Sue "but I'm also very pleased.....Delia will be delighted I'm sure. She did say that she has been very helpful and told her she could stay until Easter if she wanted to ."

"That's OK then, as I invited her to the 'gathering' on Easter Monday!" laughed Val.

"Anyway, have you any idea where my egg hiding husband is.... He came home laughing his head off last night!" added Val.

"Yes...both he and Neil definitely had some fun last night, that is for sure....I don't actually know where the eggs are so I'll have to have a look later. I think Rupert is with Neil on one of the games......I think I had better go and relieve Brian of the maps for a little while so that he can mingle ." said Sue.

"How do you think he is...Brian" asked Val " have you heard any more about Alice?"

"Not a thing" said Sue "he seems OK, but sometimes he looks as if he's far away in a world of his own....we just need to watch out for him. I'll see you in a little while" and gave her friend a hug before going to take over from Brian.

The sun continued to shine and people continued to arrive and it was clear that all was going well. The 'buzz' of chatter and laughter and children playing was wonderful for everyone so it was a bit of a shock when Sue suddenly heard a lot of shouting and looked up to see the policeman on duty running to the end of the road. She also saw Neil, Rupert and several of the dad's from school running in the same direction. She couldn't leave where she was but was anxious to find out what was going on. She managed to 'catch' Val's eye who came and took over from her whilst Sue went to find out what was happening.

By the time she caught up with the men they were walking slowly back deep in conversation, but she gathered that there had been a group of youths on motorbikes trying to push the barrier down.....

"Just thugs trying to cause a problem Sue " said Neil "don't worry, it's sorted now and young constable Bradley has asked for a couple more men to come down and assist keeping the roads clear. No harm done...."

Sue tried to put it out of her mind but she couldn't help but think that Neil wasn't telling her everything which was strange....never mind, she would ask him later.

By the end of the afternoon every cake had been sold....along with lots and lots of raffle tickets ....the stalls had sold an abundance of items.....the games had gone non stop and they had seen more people joining in than they had for a long time.

The hog roast had been started and the marquee would be transformed for the evening with fairly lights. Before she could sit down and relax Sue went to thank all the stall holders and helpers. She went to where Vicki and Gaynor were putting the 'rat' away but before she could speak Vicki said "Sue...we have had a really smashing day....thank you for involving us. I know we seemed reluctant when you asked....we didn't expect it to be like this."

"Yes" agreed Gaynor "we've had a lot of fun and we've both been saying what an amazing job you've done organising it....". Gaynor then added, rather shyly...

We're sorry we've been such cows to you Sue....especially when Alice left...it's none of our business, we know that. But if you ever want any help with anything else...just ask..."

"Well thank you....I really do appreciate that" said Sue. "Are you staying for the hog roast? You're very welcome to ."

“I’d like that” said Vicki “but I’ll have to go and sort the children out first and come back....if that’s ok?”

“Of course it is” replied Sue “we’ll be here for ages....just come when you’re ready” she added as she started to walk away, then over her shoulder smiled at them and added “it would be nice to see you in church tomorrow!”

The tables in the marquee had been re-arranged so that people could sit and eat and chat. Sue couldn’t wait to sit down. As she approached the marquee she saw Brian deep in conversation with Neil. They didn’t see her approach and she

overheard Neil telling Brian to be careful......careful about what thought Sue just as Neil looked up and said “There you are....you must be exhausted....come on, time for a drink...”

“Thanks Sue for all your hard work” added Brian.

“Come on Brian....you’ve worked hard all day as well...time for a drink and some food courtesy of Freddie” Sue told him.

“I don’t think so Sue...I need to finish my sermon for tomorrow” said Brian.

“No you don’t...you finished it the other day....I know you did....I’m not taking ‘no’ for an answer! Come and sit with us and have drink and some food.” Insisted Sue taking Brian’s arm and dragging him into the marquee so that he couldn’t refuse.

Most of the helpers had stayed along with family and friends. Freddie was being his usual charming, wonderful host and thanked Sue profusely for her wonderful organisation. He told her that he had just spoken to Billy and they had made more money than in the previous two years, so Sue was feeling very happy and thoroughly enjoyed the glasses of wine offered! The children had some of the hog roast and then Sue’s Mum and Dad took them home so that Sue and Neil could stay for a while chatting.

The camaraderie between the helpers and members of the congregation was clear. Brian stayed and definitely became more relaxed after a couple of drinks and chatted to both Vicki and Gaynor who came back for a while.

Sue completely forgot about the conversation she overheard between Neil and Brian.

Chapter 33

It was a very tired – and somewhat hung over congregation who gathered in St.

Aidan's the following morning for the Palm Sunday service but it was a much larger congregation than they had had for a while and Sue was delighted, especially as she could see that Brian seemed more relaxed this morning.

The service went well and the children gave out Palm crosses to everyone and did a little parade with large palms to one of the hymns.

In the meeting room afterwards there was a definite 'buzz' as people talked about the Easter Eggstravaganza the day before. There seemed to be quite a lot of talk about where all the eggs had been planted and she could see Neil having a little smile. Sue hadn't had the time to find them the day before and knew that they were still in place so decided to have a look for them after lunch before Neil took them down.

"You've put some in places where no one could see them, haven't you?" Sue said to Neil giving him a prod from behind.

With that Neil laughed out loud. "Well it made it much more fun!"

"Don't take them down until I've had a chance to look for them this afternoon" replied Sue as Delia came over to join them.

"Did you find all the hidden eggs yesterday Delia?" asked Sue.

"I didn't really get chance to have a look, to be honest ." replied Delia.

"Do you fancy having a look with me after lunch?" asked Sue.

"Oh, yes, that would be fun....but I must tell you" started Delia lowering her voice.

" Betty is going to stay until after Easter."

"You are joking?" responded Sue.

"No, I'm not" said Delia "but to be honest Sue, she really has been a different person... She has actually been very helpful and not at all the usual critical Betty...so in a way her staying until after Easter will help so that I can do some work and she can supervise the children – or help Jack to supervise them" laughed Delia. "Val has also invited her on Easter Monday....she was really taken with that!" Both Sue and Delia laughed knowing what Val had said to her on the phone!

"Is about 3 o'clock ok to meet" asked Sue as she started to tidy up.

"Yes that's fine" replied Val. "I'll meet you outside.......don't forget the map!"

Sue's Mum and Dad had stayed overnight and June, Sue's Mum had started the lunch by the time Sue got back from church. After a leisurely family lunch June and Derek, Sue's Mum & Dad, said they would make a move to go home as Derek was working the following day. They were coming to stay the following weekend for Easter as they had also been invited to Val's on Easter Monday. The children didn't want them to go as Grandad was always good to play with, but as they promised Easter Eggs the following week the children gave reluctant hugs and let them go home.

"Right Neil......you can sort out the washing up whilst I go on the hunt with Delia....and we better be able to find them all!" Instructed Sue.

Neil laughed and said "Look up and look down.....and that's all I'm going to tell you!"

With that Sue grabbed her jacket and went off to meet Delia leaving the children playing games and Neil clearing up the lunch dishes.

Delia was waiting for her at church when she got there.

"Have you got the map?" Delia asked. "I think I've already spotted a couple."

"Yes it's here...where have you seen some?" Sue asked.

"Look up into the holly tree......am I right? Is that an egg?" Delia enquired.

"I think it is. Neil said to look up and look down" said Sue. "Let's mark them on the map and go on the hunt....I bet it'll take us an hour or so as they put them all round the Village according to the map."

After an hour Delia and Sue had found fifty eggs, but there were three that eluded them. As they walked back towards the church Neil and the children were coming from the other direction.

"Well....have you found them all" he shouted.

"We're missing three" shouted Sue back.

As he caught up to them he checked the map and laughed. The three that they had missed were very close to church but slightly hidden by a grave.

"Come on I'll show you......" said Neil.

"Oh so easy when you show us" said Delia dismayed that they had missed them.

"I'm going to start collecting them" said Neil "will you take the children home, Sue?"

"Aw, Dad...you said that I could help" complained Adam.

"You did promise Neil" said Sue.

"Yes, I suppose I did.......OK – but don't go climbing....stay with me" instructed Neil.

"I will, I will...thanks Dad" said an excited Adam.

"You got time for a cuppa" Delia asked Sue "the children can have a play together for an hour."

"Oh yes please Auntie Delia" chimed Flora and Bobby together listening in to their Mum's conversation.

"Yes....why not. There's no school tomorrow, so there's no rush tonight" said Sue as they started to walk to Delia's.

"Did Val tell you that she would be working on Thursday so she couldn't meet up?" Sue asked Delia.

"Yes...she did mention it........that's quite unusual for Val really....she doesn't give up her Thursday very readily" said Delia "but to be truthful Sue it might have been a bit of a push for me this week as well, particularly as Mum and Gerry get back from Spain on Thursday and I said that I would collect them from the airport...and they will want to see Jack as well."

"That's fine Delia.....it's a busy week for me as well as there are all the Holy week Services to help with. But as we'll all be together on Easter Monday at Val's we can have a catch up them. I hope the weather stays nice....we can put the children outside!" Sue laughed as they approached Delia's house.

I have been meaning to ask Sue....have you heard anything about Alice?" asked Delia as they went inside.

"Not a thing" responded Sue and then remembered the conversation she had overheard Between Neil and Brian.

"Did you hear anything yesterday during the Eggstravaganza?" asked Sue.

"In what way?" asked Delia.

"Well I overheard Neil saying something to Brian about being careful....but I'm not sure what he was 'to be careful' about, and I forgot to ask Neil last night....it's probably something and nothing" said Sue thoughtfully just as Betty came into the kitchen.

"Hello Sue, love......have you recovered from all your organising yet? It was a good turn out. I understand there were a lot of visitors from 'out of town'" laughed Betty.

"I'm fine Betty, thanks. Relieved that it all went well and we made a significant amount of money......." replied Sue taking the coffee offered from Delia.

"I'll just go and see if Jack wants a coffee" said Delia leaving Sue with Betty.

"Delia tells me that you're staying over the Easter weekend, Betty" mentioned Sue.

"Yes, I am. I'm really hoping to make amends to Delia" Betty answered quietly. "I realise that I've not been very fair with her....I can see that Jack is happy and well looked after and the children are delightful....... I think after Jack's father died I was so lonely I went a little mad with grief, and I've been unfair to Delia, so I want to get things in proportion and be a good mother-in-law ...rather than the mother out-law!" Betty laughed as she said it just as Delia came back into the kitchen clearly having heard what Betty had said.

"I'll make Jack a coffee and we can have a natter whilst the children play for a while" said Delia.

After putting the world to rights and discussing how well people had got on the day before Sue said that she needed to get back as it would be a busy week – especially with the children being on holiday.

Sue gathered up her children, gave Delia and Betty hugs and shouted cheerio to Jack and made her way home with one child holding each hand.

She desperately tried to remember what it was she needed to ask Neil.................

Chapter 34

It was a busy week for the 'Three Musketeers'!

Sue was busy helping out with services in church.............Val was working on a big event due to take place over the May Bank Holiday and Delia was getting into the new job she had taken on. Jack had been helping, as it was *his* job really but once his leg was mended he would more than likely be promoted.

Easter weekend arrived along with Sue's Mum and Dad to stay.....her brother and his family were coming for dinner on Sunday, along with Neil's Mum and Dad, Lilly and Bob. Neil's parent's had moved from the village a while ago into a bungalow near the coast. It was only about a half hour drive from Neil in one direction and his sister in the other. They were both working but hoped to take early retirement in the next couple of years and do some travelling. They were 'young' for their age and both had a positive outlook on getting old and they loved their grand children! So it was a real treat to be with them all for Easter dinner. Neil's sister was on holiday and hadn't, as yet, had any children, though they all thought it was 'on the cards'!

Delia had collected her Mum and Bill from the airport and brought them to see Jack. Delia's dad had died when she was in primary school and it had been hard for both her and her Mum. June had met Bill about five years later.....just as Delia was in her teens and she resented Bill's intrusion for a while. Delia soon realised that her Mum needed someone and it was clear that Bill cared deeply for her. Bill was a patient man and tried gently to make Delia understand that he wanted to look after them both. He had also been widowed but had no children – something he regretted. So very slowly he worked on Delia until she realised that he was a good man and she warmed to him. So much so that he 'gave her away' on her wedding day and they had been firm friends ever since.

Val and Rupert were looking forward enormously to their little party on Easter Monday. They had organised caterer's and a gazebo in case the weather turned wet, though at the moment it looked good. There was plenty of room in the house but Val thought that they could put toys and games in the gazebo for the children. It could be their 'den' for the day. Once organised they went off to Rupert's parent's for Easter lunch collecting Val's Mum and Dad and sister on the way.

Chapter 35

Easter Monday dawned with a few clouds but the sun threatening to make way for a beautiful day.

Rupert and Val were up and about as the caterer's would be arriving soon after 10.30 to set up before everyone arrived for 1 o'clock.

Rupert gathered the toys together to put in the gazebo while Val got her self ready. She had been rather tired after their visit to Rupert's parents the day before. Rupert's father – Greg was always full of fun and ready with a joke or two. He had actually done an Easter egg hunt for Rupert and Val and Rupert's brother Dan and he would not take 'no ' for an answer when they protested! He had, however, bought the most beautiful chocolate creations for Nina – Rupert's Mum and Val which he presented to them when all the laughter had finished after Dan found the tiniest of plastic eggs hidden in a plant pot in the greenhouse.

The caterer's arrived as arranged and after Val had shown them where everything was she left them to hide the most brightly coloured toy eggs with a few chocolate ones, but they would be given their 'real' chocolate eggs after lunch...and when they had found all the toy ones!

"Well I think we're all done, Val" announced Rupert as he pulled his wife into his arms.

"How do you feel?"

"I'm fine....it will be so good to have everyone here" smiled Val "I'm quite excited about the announcement" she added.

Rupert hugged her tight...."I know this sounds daft...but I'm really quite nervous!"

Val laughed and hugged him back just as the door bell rang.

“Ooh, someone is eager” said Rupert.....”I’ll bet any money it’s Sue and Neil with the children. They’ll be wanting to start the Easter egg hunt” he laughed as he went to answer the door.

As Rupert answered the door Neil started to apologise.....”I’m sorry pal...the kids were desperate to get here!”

“Uncle Rupert” shouted all three of them at once “when can we do the egg hunt?”

“Egg hunt?” answered Rupert keeping his face straight “what egg hunt?”

“Aw...Uncle Rupert, we always have an egg hunt here” announced Adam.

As three pairs of eyes looked beseechingly and Val joined them at the door,

Rupert couldn’t contain himself any more. He laughed.

“What’s going on here?” asked Val.

“Aw Auntie Val” said Adam “Uncle Rupert says he doesn’t know anything about an egg hunt!”

Val slapped Rupert on the arm “Oh you big tease....take no notice you three. Of course there’s an Easter Egg hunt but you can’t do it until the other’s arrive....anyway, what are you doing standing on the doorstep...come on in.”

Sue gave Val a hug as Rupert shook Neil’s hand. They always did this even if they had only seen each other a few days before.

They took their coats off and hung them in the little cloakroom off the hallway.

“Oh my goodness” exclaimed Sue as she saw all that the caterer’s were doing.

“You know Val, we could all have brought something...you didn’t have to go to all this trouble!”

“Well it is our wedding anniversary and we wanted to make it a bit special this year” replied Val as the door bell went again.

“I’ll go” shouted Rupert.

For the next half an hour the door bell kept ringing, there’s were lots of hugs and the noise level rose considerably with chatter and laughter as everyone tried to ’catch up’ with each other.

Rupert volunteered Neil to help him with the drinks as Jack was still on crutches. The children were getting desperate to do the Easter Egg hunt so Val gave them all a little basket each and the adults counted them down from ten before they ran off into the garden.

As the adults watched and listened to the children’s excitement they had little chats amongst themselves.

After about twenty minutes five smiling children came running in with baskets full of little plastic eggs and a few small chocolate ones. Adam had helped the younger ones to find some and Val gave him a big hug. She really adored her God child.

“Well let me see” said Rupert “who has the most?”

The children tipped there baskets onto the carpet for Rupert to count.

“I think they’re all about the same....what does everyone else think” he asked.

“Absolutely...definitely....without a doubt” was the cheer from the adults as they all chuckled at the eager faces of the five children.

Val had disappeared but at that moment came into the lounge with five huge chocolate eggs. The children’s eyes were like saucers and whilst the men smiled at their reaction a few tears could be seen amongst the older generation!

"Right you lot....there's an egg each for you but they are not to be touched until after lunch and only then if your mums agree to you opening them. Deal?" asked Val.

"Oh yes please Auntie Val" came the response from them all.

"Ok then.....it's time for lunch ."

The caterer's had laid out the most amazing spread in the dining room for people to help themselves . There were a few special things for the children who obediently went and sat in the little 'den' as Val liked to call it. It was really a small cosy room where she liked to work sometimes.

The adults all came in chatting away. It was good to see Jack's mum talking away to Chrissy Melker – her bosses wife, though they were also good friends.

June and Bill were chatting away to Sue's Mum & Dad and Rupert was having a good chat with Jack whilst Sue was having, what looked like an in depth conversation with Delia.

Val felt so lucky.....everyone she really cared about were under her roof today.

"Earth to Val" she heard Sue say. "Come and get some of this gorgeous feast before the fellas scoff it all ."

"I was miles away" smiled Val at her two friends .

"Yes, we could see that" smiled Delia in return.

The three friends filled their plates and went to sit together in the garden where the sun was now shining and the garden looked beautiful with the colour of spring flowers everywhere . They chatted about the Easter Eggstravaganza and what a success it was.......and Delia told them that the man who had been shot by Jason Chadwick - the man who had hit Jack's car, had died, so Chadwick was now on a murder charge.

“Sergeant Brookes phoned to tell us that the court case was being prepared and that they had accessed the footage from Jack’s car, which proved conclusively that not only had he been speeding but he was on the wrong side of the road ” added Delia.

“I don’t think that young man will be getting out of prison for a very long time .”

“I seem to remember hearing soon after the shooting, that there was a witness to the shooting” said Val “but I haven't heard any more.”

“Apparently there is a witness” replied Delia “but it’s being kept very hush, hush for some reason....but it seems this Chadwick is involved in all sorts of things, so it could be one of his ‘gang’ giving evidence to save themselves ” she added.

The three women sat and chatted whilst they ate and stopped occasionally to look back into the house when they heard loud raucous laughter .

“I don’t know what’s going on in there” said Val “but we seem to be missing

something .”

“If I know Neil and Jack and Rupert when they get together with Neil’s dad and Bill it’ll probably be to do with football!” added Sue.

A few minutes later the children came out looking for their Mums.

“Have you had enough to eat?“ asked Val.

“Yes thank you” came the reply from them all.

“Please can we have some more cake later Auntie Val?” asked Maisie.

“Of course you can” replied Val before Delia or Sue could respond.

"Now....if you go into the gazebo at the bottom of the garden you'll find lots of things to do...there are some games, some crafty stuff and bits and pieces....go and help yourselves" Val told them as the children ran off to find where the goodies were.

"Am I imagining it, or can I see Rupert with bottles of champagne?" asked Sue.

Before Val could answer Rupert shouted to them to join everyone inside, and Val moved at lightening speed before Delia or Sue could ask further.

"Something's afoot here I think" observed Delia.

"Hmm.....I think you're right" agreed Sue as the two women walked together into the lounge.

Val and Rupert's house was a lovely, modern detached house where the bi-fold doors on the conservatory went straight out onto the garden which looked superb with glorious flowers blooming all around. Val always laughed when they commented as she wasn't really a gardener – although she would tidy up a little, and Rupert was always too busy or tired at the weekend, so their lovely garden was down to a retired chap that they paid to keep it tidy. They all agreed it was worth every penny!

As the two women walked into the lounge they knew that something was going on and looked at each other puzzled.

Rupert had a crystal glass in his hand and was tapping it gently with a spoon to get everyone's attention amongst the loud chattering that was going on.

"Can I have your attention everyone , please" said Rupert in a very loud voice.

Lots of shushing ensued...as one shushed, another shushed the other and they all ended up in fits of laughter.

"Quiet please, quiet please" said Rupert in a very authoritative voice, and this time everyone quietened down.

“Thank you all for coming today to help us celebrate our wedding anniversary” started Rupert as he put his hand out to Val to stand beside him...

“Val and I have an announcement to make..........”

At this point you could have heard a pin drop as all their friends and family wondered what was going on.

Rupert’s Mum was almost holding her breath as she knew that Rupert had been offered a job in Dubai.......she was now silently praying that they weren’t going to live there........

“Shall I tell them” Val asked Rupert, ”or are you going to do it?”

“Well whatever it is will you pleeeeeze tell us....I can’t stand the suspense anymore!” said Neil laughing.

“We’re going to have a baby” said Rupert “Well Val’s having the baby obviously.....”

And before he could say anymore both Val’s Mum and Rupert’s burst into tears accompanied by them both saying in unison “we’re going to be Grandma’s” at which everyone laughed and the words of congratulations flowed from them all with Neil and Jack shaking Rupert’s hand, and his dad patting him on the back.

“This is a celebration” said Rupert as he started handing out glasses of champagne with the help of Neil.

Delia and Sue were quite shell shocked as they had always thought their friend was so career minded that children weren’t on her agenda . They both got up and went to Val and gave her the most enormous group hug they could muster.

“Why didn’t you tell us” demanded Sue “we are sooooo happy for you – it is what you want?” she added quietly.

Val pulled them both away from the others.

"You have no idea how long we've been hoping for a baby" beamed Val "you know my periods were always irregular at school....well it's continued for ever! I've seen gynaecologists on and off for a while but they couldn't find a proper reason for the irregularities......so we've just let nature take its course........... I can't tell you how much I've been wanting to tell you, but if you'd known how much we wanted a baby you'd have been asking and I don't think I could have coped with the situation. We told no one at all so that there wasn't any 'group' disappointment"

"I am absolutely delighted for you" said Sue

"and so am I" added Val.

"So when are we going baby shopping" asked Val and all three women laughed and hugged and cried at the same time.

"I must speak to the Grandmas to be" said Val giving her friends another hug.

"Well, I never expected that today" said Delia smiling.

"Neither did I" agreed Sue "but I am so delighted for them....they'll make a lovely mum and dad....I can see Rupert now wanting to push the pram!"

Delia laughed and agreed then added "We'll have to start planning a baby shower for her ."

"Yes, that would be lovely....she didn't say when it was due.....let's go and ask" remarked Sue.

Val was talking to both her mum and Rupert's who were both laughing and crying at the same time and giving Val a hug in between.

"I think we should probably leave it for a while so that those two can get used to the idea of being grannies" laughed Sue and went to sit with June, Delia's Mum.

"Hi June...how are you, how was your holiday?" asked Sue .

"Hello Sue....well that was unexpected I think, don't you?" said June sipping her champagne.

"It certainly was June.....but I am so happy for them" said Sue.

"Oh yes...me too" added June.

"Come on then globetrotter.....what sort of a holiday have you had...you've been away weeks" asked Sue.

"We've had a wonderful time Sue. The weather was glorious – but then you would expect that in Spain, and we bumped into a few old friends that we've seen there before....so it's been lovely......but I've missed Delia and the children. We wanted to come straight back when we heard about Jack's accident, but Delia insisted that we didn't as there was nothing that we could do.......but now we're back and Jack's home I'm hoping that she'll let us help with the children, especially as she's taken on this new job" remarked June.

"I'm sure that she will really appreciate your help particularly as Betty is going home next week" replied Sue.

Lowering her voice June said to Sue "that's a bit of a turn up for the books.....Betty, if you take my meaning?"

"You can say that again" replied Sue "You know the story of Val giving her 'what for' on the phone......." June nodded.

"Well it clearly did the trick and made her think.....we kept waiting for her to have a hissy fit....but it's never happened, and more than that she even helped with the Easter Eggstravaganza!"

"Wow....now that is something...talking of which, you know that Deacon or archdeacon , or something like that –

his name's Dennis" started June "the one who flirts with everyone under 90?"

"Oh, you've heard, have you?" said Sue.

"Heard, heard what....no...I was going to tell you about us seeing him in Spain" said June.

"IN SPAIN" said Sue.

"Yes....he's running a bar with his partner" replied June.

"RUNNING A BAR IN SPAIN WITH ALICE — you've got to be kidding" said Sue rather shocked.

"Alice.....who's Alice?" asked June.....

For the next few minutes Sue told June what had gone on some weeks before and that Alice had been seen leaving with Dennis the dreadful.

"No, no Sue.....there was no woman there...........Dennis was running the bar with his 'partner' .....Jason.....Jeremy .....something like that.........Oh no...I remember : GORDON! Yes, that's it!" June laughed......"I'll tell you why I remember....the bar is called 'The Gay Gordon ' and she laughed again....at which Sue laughed as well.

"Are you telling me that Dennis the Dreadful is running a bar with a 'gay' friend?" asked Sue.

"No Sue.......Dennis is running the bar with his PARTNER- Gordon! And my oh my, you should see some of his shirts.............gaudy doesn't come into it....you can probably see them from outer space they are so loud" June was laughing not so much at what she had said but at Sue's face.

"Sue.....close your mouth you'll be catching flies" laughed June.

"I can't take in what you are telling me June.....Dennis GAY.........he was always flirting with all the ladies regardless of age....!" commented Sue .

"And that's probably why he did it.......he was completely harmless" added June.

"Wow.....this is a lot to take in.......but are you sure that you didn't see Alice......so you remember her from some of the church 'doos' we've had?" asked Sue.

"I do remember her Sue....a lovely young woman and totally besotted with that husband of hers.......I find it hard to believe that she left him............but she certainly didn't leave him for Dennis!" and June chuckled again at the very thought.

"We actually stayed and had a drink at the bar......we enjoyed ourselves......they're both very funny....Gordon and Dennis. They were really pulling the crowds in as they were doing meals as well."

"I'm really shocked at what you are telling me June.......he's an Archdeacon......but the puzzle is :where is Alice if she's not with Dennis?" said Sue as Neil overheard...."what are you shocked about....Not these two taking the plunge at long last on the baby front.....it's great news isn't it?"

"It certainly is" said Rupert as he came round filling the empty glasses with more champagne.

"I can't stop smiling.......Val's been longing to be a Mum and I am over the moon at the idea of being a dad!"

"Wait til you have to get up in the early hours for feeding and changing" said Neil.

"OY.....who did most of the feeding and changing in the middle of the night mister!" responded Sue indignantly. Neil laughed....."Well you did most of it I admit......"

"I'm sure we'll cope somehow" said Rupert....." and if we can't I'll just ring you guys up" he said laughing.

"When is this baby due anyway?" asked Sue "you've not told us ."

“I’ll get Val to give you all the details......Val .....details over here please” laughed Rupert as Val came over to her friend.

“When is this baby due....you never told us” asked Sue.

“Ah well....” replied Val “I’m not actually sure of the date....sometime late September or October I think. I should know better next week. You know when I couldn’t meet you for our usual Thursday gathering last week?” said Val as Delia joined them and they both nodded “Well it was because I was at the clinic having the pregnancy confirmed. They will do a scan next week and then we’ll have a proper date. I’m sorry I couldn't tell you why I couldn't meet you, but I wasn’t sure myself then......it was more suspicion .”

“So that’s why you haven’t been feeling well these last few weeks!” said Sue knowingly.

“I think you’re right....but I honestly had no idea......I didn’t even dare hope so that I wouldn’t be disappointed” replied Val wistfully.

“Well....it should go without saying that Sue and I are here for you should you need any gory details about giving birth......or even how to change a nappy” laughed Delia.

“Now, come on“ added Delia “I think it’s time for cake, and looking at those children I think they are desperate to open great big Easter Eggs”.

Chapter 36

The next couple of weeks were fairly uneventful. The children went back to school after the Easter holiday with Adam going into his last term before going to high school in September.

Betty had gone home following the three women taking her to 'Mugs with Hugs' for lunch and where she promised not to leave it too long before she came again!

Delia had already said that the relationship had completely changed since Betty's conversation with Val and that even Diane – Jack's sister had noticed a change for the better.

A few days after Betty had gone home Delia rang Sue.

"We've got the date for the court hearing Sue".

"Is this the preliminary or the main event?" asked Sue.

"Well it would seem that Chadwick has already been sent to crown court from the magistrates...so this is the main event as you say " Delia told her.

"When is it Delia....will you have to attend?" Sue asked.

"Jack will be called to give evidence and I really want to be with him...it starts in just over a fortnight" Delia told her.

"If there's anything we can do....or if you want us to be with you Delia, just say the word...I rather think that Neil may want to be there anyway" said Sue.

"I was wondering if between you and my Mum you would help with the children when we're at court?" asked Delia.

"That's not a problem Delia....I've told you before that I can always collect them and feed them......there's no need to ask" responded Sue.

"I know that Sue, but I don't want you thinking that I'm taking advantage .....you're such a good friend" stated Delia.

"Don't be daft....I enjoy them being here.....anyway........whilst you're on we need to think about organising a baby shower for Val. Shall I have a word with Lynn and Nina — the grannies to be?" Sue said laughing.

"That's a good idea and also, Val should know next week when the baby is due, so we can plan better once we know " replied Val.

"Shall I let Val know about the court date....I rather think that Rupert may want to be there as well?" added Sue.

"Yes, if you don't mind...I've got quite a lot of work on this week......are we meeting on Thursday as usual?" asked Val.

"Absolutely.....I'll see you then " and Sue put the phone down.

Sue phoned Val once the children were in bed that evening.

"How are you feeling mummy to be" laughed Sue down the phone.

"I'm feeling much better, just tired.....I think I might be further on than I realise as the morning sickness seems to have gone away" Val told her friend.

"That's good" responded Sue "but be aware that it could come back later on..."

"Oh thanks for that....what joy!" laughed Val.

"Anyway" said Sue "I rang to tell you about the court case....Delia rang this morning to say that it's in just over a fortnight. I told her that Neil would probably want to be there and I suspected that Rupert might want to as well "

"I think you're right....hang on a minute...I'll ask him...he's upstairs measuring the nursery for furniture...bless....."

Sue smiled as she heard Val shout Rupert upstairs . She could hear the conversation and then Rupert came to the phone.....

“Hi Sue.....is Neil going to the trial?” Rupert asked.

“Hi Rupert...well he’s hoping to if he can swop one or two jobs about...he’s quite busy at the moment but wanted to give Jack some moral support.....and I expect he wants to see what is going on!” Sue told him.

“Ok..well I’ll speak to Neil in a day or two and see how my schedule fits with his...... I’ll hand you back to Val....see you soon”

Val came back on the phone...

“I think both Delia and Jack will feel better once this is all sorted out, don’t you?” Val asked Sue.

“Yes, I do.....it’s not something that Jack will forget in a hurry....but remember this lad is up on a murder charge as well and from what Delia has said he seems to be involved in all sorts of criminal activities particularly drugs and stealing cars... Such a young man to be so bad......” said Sue. “ Anyway, mummy to be....I’ll let you go and get your rest .”

“Are we meeting as usual on Thursday?” asked Val.

“Oh yes please....we’ve not been able to do that for a few weeks so it will be nice....I’ll tell Delia to keep her morning free. I’ll see you on Thursday...sleep well” laughed Sue.

“And you...see you Thursday Sue....thanks for ringing ” and Val and Sue put their phones down together.

Chapter 37

Once Sue had got the children off to school on Thursday morning she went home to get some general jobs done before setting off to meet Val and Delia at 'Mugs with Hugs' . Sue realised just how much she had missed their weekly ritual as it was four weeks since they had been able to meet on a Thursday.

Sue was the first to arrive with Val arriving two minutes later. They had been there for about ten minutes when Delia arrived looking flustered.

"You OK?" asked Val.

"Yes...I'm sorry I'm late....we had Sgt Brookes on the phone just as I was coming out. He wanted to know how Jack was and to say that we would hear fairly soon the date for the trial. He told us that it's not looking good at all for this Chadwick character as more evidence against him had been found in another case! Anyway, enough of that...we'll have a belly full of it once the trial starts........now...are we ordering or what? " smiled Delia.

Delia and Sue ordered their usual but Val decided on a caffeine free green tea to which both Sue and Delia pulled faces! But Val did decide on her regular cookie!

"When is you ante-natal appointment Val?" asked Delia.

"It's tomorrow afternoon.....I'm going to that new posh clinic outside Willbury" said Val.

"Ooh get you.....posh clinic eh" laughed Sue.

"Well the thing is Rupert has private health care with his work and he said that we might as well take advantage.....but I will persuade him that the local GP and midwives are fine.....I'm just going tomorrow so that I can get an accurate date and book in for some 3D scan or something that they do" said Val.

"Ring us tomorrow when you have an accurate date" said Delia.

"Yes, I'll do that" agreed Val.

******

Soon after Sue had got Flora and Bobby to bed the following evening she answered the phone to hear Val's voice.....

"Hi Sue....are you busy this evening?" asked Val

"Well I've just got the littlies to bed...Adam is up but watching TV....why...is something the matter.......everything's alright with the baby?" asked Sue.

"Oh yes, yes...baby's ok, but I need to speak to you and I wondered if you could come here? And possibly bring Delia as well?" asked Val

"Hang on a minute while I speak to Neil ...." Sue came back a few minutes later...

"I can be round in about half an hour or so....." said Sue.

"That would be good......will you ring Delia and see if she's free?" asked Val.

"Yes of course.....Val...are you sure you're ok?" asked a very concerned Sue.

Honestly I'm fine....but I need to speak to you" said Val.

"Ok....hopefully Delia will be free and we'll see you later" replied Sue.

Sue rang Delia and told her about the phone call. Delia was as concerned as Sue and said that she could be ready in twenty minutes or so once the children were settled and asked Sue to pick her up on the way to which Sue readily agreed to.

Twenty five minutes later Sue had collected Delia and they were on there way to Val's, which was only a five minute drive.

"What on earth do you think is wrong?" Delia asked Sue.

"I'm really not sure....but she got me worried even though she said she was ok and the baby....but she was most insistent that she wanted to see us...and she was at the clinic today" said Sue just as they pulled up outside Val and Rupert's house.

"We'll soon find out" said Sue as they got out of the car.

Val had been watching for them through the front window and she opened the door as soon as they got out of the car.

As Sue and Delia got to the door Val exclaimed "It's OK....I'm fine and the baby's fine......come on in....Rupert had just put the coffee on."

Delia and Sue took off their coats and gave them to Val who ushered them into the conservatory. It was a lovely evening and getter lighter by the day as summer approached.

"Val, you've got us really worried....what is the matter?" asked Sue just as Rupert appeared with a tray of coffee and biscuits for them.

"I'll let you tell them" said Rupert "shout if you want me, I'll be in the study" as he bent to give Val a kiss, and with that he left the three friends together.

Delia and Sue looked at Val expectantly waiting for her to tell them what was going on.

"You know that I went to that private clinic outside Willbury for the ante-natal clinic" began Val....

"Yes, you said that you were going yesterday" Delia said.

"Well.....that was the second visit. I went originally to have the check up when I hadn't been feeling well....do you remember badgering me into going to the doctor's Sue?"

Sue nodded in agreement as Val continued...."I was there for quite a while the first time I went...it must be three weeks or so ago now, and because they thought I was pregnant I went to the ante-natal area to have some tests done. While I was there – I was reading a magazine and had looked up – I saw someone that looked familiar to me but couldn't for the life of me place her."

"Have you remembered who it was?" asked Sue

"Well that's the thing. I saw her again yesterday in the ante-natal clinic. She couldn't see me because of the way the rooms are laid out, but I had spotted her. It took me a while to work out who she was until I saw Brian."

Brian....?" asked Delia. "Brian who?"

"BRIAN....your vicar Brian.......Brian Barton and Alice" declared Val.

"Brian.......and ALICE?" said Sue going quite pale. "You must be mistaken Val.......why......how........I can't take this in."

"I'm telling you Sue, it was Brian and Alice. She was wearing a short brunette wig which is why I couldn't place her at first. And she is pregnant Sue...." Val told her.

"I've not made a mistake.....Rupert saw Brian as well, but thankfully Brian didn't see him!"

Both Delia and Sue were absolutely stunned and didn't know what to say for a few minutes.

"So.....what on earth is going on?" said Delia. "All this with Dennis.....and the suitcase......and that nosey woman who does the flowers....what's her name......"

"Brenda" Sue said quietly. "I don't know what to think.....you know that your Mum saw Dennis running a bar in Spain with his gay partner" Sue said to Delia.

"She didn't tell me that" replied Delia.

"No. She didn't mention it to me either" retorted Val....."but then to be fair there was a lot going on when we were all together on Easter Monday."

“I can’t take this in” said Sue. “Why would Brian pretend that Alice had left him and with Dennis......when in fact she’s pregnant and he’s at the clinic with her....it doesn’t make any sense.”

“Now can you see why I couldn’t tell you this on the phone” said Val “it all seems rather bizarre .”

The three women were all drinking coffee and contemplating what had been said when Rupert came in.

“Looking at your faces, Val has told you who we saw at the clinic yesterday” commented Rupert.

“Yes....she has” agreed Delia. “It’s very strange......there must be something behind it all.........I mean....why would Alice want to keep her pregnancy secret for one thing......and why would Brian keep it to himself.....?”

“Hmmm” Sue said quietly. “Can I ask you all something?”

“Yes, of course” Val, Rupert and Delia chimed together.

“Please will you keep this strictly amongst ourselves for the time being. I’m sure there’s more to this ..... NO. I’m absolutely certain that there is more to this and until we find out WHAT is going on, I think we should keep it to ourselves. There must be a very good reason for Brian to let everyone think that Alice has left him.”

“I think you’re right Sue” agreed Rupert. “I like Brian and I don’t see him as deceitful at all....so there must be a good reason.....well I’ll go back to the study and let you girls have a baby gossip” he said laughing which is exactly what they went on to do for the next hour or so.

Chapter 38

When Sue got home she checked on the children who were sound asleep then dragged Neil away from the TV and told him what she had learned from Val.

“There must be some mistake” said Neil “Brian would never pretend that Alice has left him....especially if she’s pregnant .”

“I know....that’s what I thought” agreed Sue. “Whatever you do Neil, don’t breathe a word of this to anyone.....but I will find out what’s going on. But until I do.....not a word to anyone .”

“No....I agree Sue...there’s more to this....but I can’t help smiling at you telling me that Dennis the demon Archdeacon is gay............who’d have thought it” said Neil laughing. “It might be worth a trip to Spain to see his shirts!”

With them both laughing and Sue sorting out the children’s school clothes for the following morning, they agreed to be particularly careful what they say in front of the children until this is all sorted out.

The following day Sue had agreed to update Neil’s accounts as he had just

completed a big job and needed to make sure that all his invoices were ready. Sue couldn’t help thinking about what Val had told them the previous evening.

She was fairly sure that Brian would be in that evening so decided that she would call and see him on church business......there was always something to discuss or sort out.

When Neil popped in for lunch she told him what she had planned and Neil agreed that they should tell Brian that they knew Alice was in the area.

Once the children were settled Sue walked the fifteen minutes through the village to the vicarage. Brian opened the door almost as soon as the bell has been rung.

"Hello Sue...what a nice surprise...you OK?" asked Brian.

"Yes...I'm fine. Are you busy? I've got a few things I'd like to go through with you" replied Sue .

"Nothing that can't wait....come on in...I'll put the kettle on" said Brian cheerfully.

Sue went into Brian's neat but comfortable office/study while Brian made them tea which he brought in on a tray with two mugs of tea and some biscuits on a plate which he told Sue to help herself to.

"Right. What have you got for me?" asked Brian.

Sue went through a few of the church bits and pieces for a few minutes....and things which usually she wouldn't bother him with but that they sorted out together in a few minutes. Then she looked at Brian and said..... "Ok Brian...that was all a bit of a pretence....rather like what's going on here ."

"What do you mean Sue?" asked Brian looking puzzled.

"I mean ALICE.....what is going on? Both you and Alice have been seen at the ante- natal clinic out side Willbury.......so.....I'll ask you again.....WHAT. IS. GOING. ON?"

A very pale Brian looked long and hard at Sue and then for the next forty minutes he told Sue everything.

"Would you like another drink Sue?" he eventually asked as he could see Sue taking it all in.

"Well ....yes, I certainly would....but not tea" smiled Sue "I think after what you've just told me I need a stiff drink!"

Brian got up and came back a couple of minutes later with two brandy's which they both knocked back in record time.

“I know that I don’t need to ask you to keep this to yourself? “ asked Brian.

Sue nodded her head silently.

“But now that you know Sue......I need help from you and Neil.....would you be willing to assist?”

“That goes without saying Brian....whatever you need us to do “ Sue told him and for the next hour they went through everything that would be necessary.

Chapter 39

The next few weeks passed by uneventfully. The weather was getting warmer, the children were enjoying being outside after school and Sue, Val and Delia continued with their Thursday morning gatherings in ' Mugs with Hugs'.

The 'Three Muskateers' had gathered at 'Mugs with hugs' the Thursday before the May bank holiday half term break.

"How's Jack doing now that he's back in work?" asked Sue as Val brought over the drinks to the table.

"He's having to take his time but he seems glad to be doing something constructive"

replied Val. "It seems likely that his promotion will be confirmed in the next day or two" she added.

"How will that affect your job Delia?" asked Val.

"Well....they've offered me the job full time now that Jack has agreed to this new role......I'm just not sure......" said Val slowly.

"What's holding you back?" asked Val puzzled. "I thought you were really enjoying it".

"That's the problem really.....I am!" stated Delia.

Both Sue and Val looked at each other and then at Delia .

"Why is that a problem?" Sue ventured to ask.

Delia took a deep breath before responding. "I feel that I should be home when the children get home and be able to do all the household stuff as well......and quite frankly I can't do it all......so I have to make a choice " she sighed.

"Delia" started Sue "You should be glad that you've been given this opportunity. You are a clever woman and should grab it with both hands. The children are used to you working and are probably the better for it. You know that I will always collect them as I have no plans to go back full time......what with doing Neil's books....church stuff.....and the odd day supply, I'm more than contented being at home........I'm always busy!"

"On top of that" piped up Val "I'll be at home for quite a while before long. I've decided to take a year off work when the baby comes, so I can muck in as well!"

"Look, think about it. We're both here and can help whenever, and you said yourself that they will be flexible if it helps you to decide. You are not going to get many companies offering that today" added Sue.

"Also" Val added "you could always get someone to do a couple of hours cleaning and ironing for you so that when you get to the weekend you can enjoy the children without thinking about school uniforms!"

The three women laughed together and Delia knew that she had real treasures in these two friends .

"When do they need your answer by?" asked Val.

"I've got a week to decide" answered Delia.

"How does Jack feel about it?" asked Sue.

"To be truthful he's all up for it.....he's more or less said the same to me as you have and I don't think he wants to lose me from the company either, which is rather heart warming" smiled Delia. "Anyway....I've got a few days before I make a decision. Now.... little mummy to be.....tell us how you are and how you've been getting on at ante-natal classes" Delia directed at Val.

"So far so good" smiled a very radiant Val "the consultant and midwife I see are lovely....very reassuring....they're lovely. I just hope it will be the same midwife when the baby comes......I feel comfortable with her ."

"Have they given you a proper date yet?" asked Sue "I know they were humming and harring"

“It looks like the end of September beginning of October, but I don’t think they’ll let me go over what with me being an ‘older’ first time mum!”

Sue and Delia both laughed at this.

“Don’t laugh!” said Val indignantly. “Some of the women I see are mere girls....honestly, some of them look as if they’ve just left school.”

“They probably have” agreed Sue.“Anyway, we need to sort our your baby shower. Has your mum got back to you with a date yet, or is she galavanting about again?”

“I’ll get her to ring you....that might be easier than me trying to pin her down“ said Val.

Whilst they were chatting about the baby shower and eating their usual cookies Brenda, the women from church who does the flowers came in with another woman and sat at a nearby table clearly deep in conversation which could be heard as it was unusually quiet for a Thursday.

“I told you, I told you“ Brenda could be heard saying “I saw the Bishop there.....I was passing on my bike.....I bet he’s going to be moved on........I mean, it’s not right is it, a vicar’s wife running off with the Archdeacon like that.“

Delia and Val looked at Sue at the same time and almost had to hold her down.

“Don’t say anything Sue“ said Val “not yet.....just listen and let’s see what else she comes out with.”

Sue couldn’t speak as she was so outraged but agreed to be quiet for the moment. Brenda had her back to Sue and hadn’t seen her when she came in as she was so engrossed in gossiping to her friend!

“I said at the beginning she was too young for that Vicar....and too pretty by far...I wouldn’t be surprised if she’d been carrying on soon after they were married” added Brenda.

Just as Sue was about to burst a blood vessel, Kathy the owner of Mugs with Hugs who had heard all this diatribe about Brian and Alice walked over to the table where Brenda and her friend were seated.

Before Kathy could speak Brenda said "Oh, there you are. We'll have two latte's."

"Not in here you won't" replied Kathy.

Looking very stunned Brenda said in a loud voice "What do you mean....not in here!"

As Val, Sue and Delia watched with interest Kathy continued......."I mean exactly as I have said : NOT. IN. HERE. You are a MEAN. SPITEFUL. NASTY woman and how you DARE to go to that church every week and smile at that lovely Vicar when behind his back you are poisoning his name and that of his wife. NOW...GET.OUT. AND DON'T COME BACK!"

With that Val, Sue and Delia erupted in spontaneous applause. Brenda turned to see who was applauding and went puce in the face when she saw Sue. She couldn't get out of the cafe quickly enough.

"Well done Kathy" said Val "you did us proud ."

"She is a nasty woman with a very dangerous tongue. I've heard her before casting aspersions about people, but I am not prepared to have it in here. I like Brian and whilst we don't know what has happened to Alice I really do not think that Brenda , or anyone else should be going round making these comments. If I were you Sue I would stop her doing the flowers in church because it just gives her the idea that she is important and she does no favours for the church, or people like you who work so hard for the village" concluded Kathy.

"Thanks Kathy" said Sue"I was about to go for her myself when you went over.....I think I might have throttled her though" she said laughing.

“I could see Val and Delia trying to keep you calm” Kathy smiled “and I didn’t want blood on the floor” at which they all laughed.

“I’ll go and get you all another drink — on the house, and I’ll join you for five minutes if that’s ok so that Val can tell me her baby news” Kathy said.

Val, Delia and Sue all chimed up together “that would be lovely!”

Chapter 40

The May half term week was a beautiful sunny week and as Delia had taken the week off, she went on a few outings with Sue, and on a trip to the zoo Val joined them.

"Well I might as well get used to these lovely children's outings" she commented when Sue suggested that she join them. In truth, Val was over the moon to be included and couldn't wait until she had her baby to push in a buggy with them all.

Adam, Sue's oldest boy and Val's godson was really looking after her and making sure she didn't do too much. Sue and Delia smiled at the way he fussed over Val who he absolutely adored.

It was busy at the zoo but they managed to see most of the animals, many who were being very docile in the heat and spraying themselves with water to keep cool.

Sue took the children to the reptile house which Delia was keen to avoid as she really wasn't at all keen on snakes. Val was ready for a sit down at this point so Delia and Val went to find the cafe and sort out drinks while Sue took the children reptile looking!

Thankfully just as Delia and Val walked into the very large, very busy cafe a family vacated a table and Val sat down with a sigh "Oh thank goodness for that! I am more than ready for a sit down."

"The further along you get" Delia told her "the more tired you will feel and you'll want to sit down a lot more ....and don't forget" added Delia laughing "you're not a spring chicken anymore ."

"Ok, ok you don't need to rub it in" said Val good humouredly.

"Don't need to rub what in" asked Sue having heard the last comment as the children ran towards them.

"Oh I was just saying that I was ready for a sit down and Delia here was commenting on my age!!" Val told her at which Sue smiled and shook her head knowing that Delia was 'winding' their friend up with her teasing. She knew that Delia was as delighted as her that Val was pregnant and was excited about the baby's arrival.

"So....what are we having to drink? I've brought a packed lunch if anyone is hungry? But I'll go and order drinks " invited Sue.

After a shipping order of fizzy drinks for the children and tea for the ladies the children went to sit on the grass just outside the cafe and took some food with them.

"I'm sure food goes straight to Adam's feet" commented Sue. "He can't seem to stop eating!"

"He's probably having a growth spurt" replied Delia.

"Well I hope he stops 'spurting' before he eats us out of house and home" laughed Sue.

They were all quiet for a few minutes whilst they drank their tea and ate a sandwich.

Delia broke the silence...."I've decided to take the job".

"So you've made the decision?" asked Val.

"Jack and I had a long talk about it the other evening. He said that these opportunities don't come along very often and the company really wants to keep me, so they are prepared to be a bit flexible with timings etc." Delia told them.

"I'd like to be able to take them to school in a morning, but I may need help collecting them at the end of the day" she added.

"Look Delia, you know that I will always collect them when I collect Flora and Bobby, so don't worry about that" Sue told her.

“I don’t want you to feel that I’m taking advantage of you though” replied Delia.

“Don’t be ridiculous.....what are friends for you silly thing. I’m quite happy doing what I do ....so I won’t be going back to full time employment any time soon” said Sue “I have loads to keep me busy and don’t forget that I do Neil’s books.....honestly Delia....it’s fine. If you need me to help just say.”

“Thanks Sue. I really do appreciate it.” Delia told her.

“Hey...don’t forget me!” Val piped up. “I’ll be around for a while once I’ve had the baby.......and when I do go back to work it will only be part time .”

“Have you decided that already?“ asked Delia.

“Well, more or less. I need to work it out with Rodney....but we think we’ll be able to sort something out.” replied Val.

“Anyway” said Delia lowering her voice “we’ve had notification from the police about the court case.”

“You have?” both Val and Sue said together.

“Yes. It starts in three weeks time. Jack will be called as a witness to confirm that the dash cam footage was from his car etc. etc. But it seems that the charge against him for the dangerous driving is minor to the main charge of murder and supplying drugs and a whole host of other things. We don’t really know the full extent of his criminal activities, and in truth, I’m not sure that I want to. But he really sounds a bad lot.....and he’s only in his twenties.”

Val and Delia listened carefully but didn’t say anything and didn’t make eye contact.

Delia continued.....”I will take time off work for the case as I want to support Jack, and I think his mother will come down for it......”

Sue cleared her throat before saying, "I'm sure Neil plans to be there for support.."

"Oh yes, Rupert will be as well, I'm sure" added Val.

If Delia noticed that Sue and Val hadn't looked at each other during this exchange, she didn't say anything. They had finished their drinks just as Flora and Maisie came running in asking if they could have ice cream.

"Well I think that is a possibility" said Val laughing. "I'll get them."

"No. No, you won't" said Delia "I'll get them....you stay there for a few more minutes."

"I'll do that as long as you let me pay for them" said a very determined Val as she went to her purse to give the money to Delia. Delia graciously accepted the money knowing that there was no point in arguing with her and took the hands of the girls to go for ice cream.

Val looked at Sue and neither of them said a word.

Chapter 41

The next couple of weeks were fairly uneventful. The children were enjoying new projects in school and the weather had remained kind which meant that they could all go for walks in the evening with the children before going to bed. Friday walks were particularly enjoyable for Neil and Jack as they often stopped at the village pub for a drink! On one occasion Brian was persuaded to join them on his way home from a visit to a parishioner.

On a beautiful balmy Friday evening the week before the trial, Rupert had joined Neil and Jack as the 'girls' had decided to have a bit of a pamper party whilst the children had decided on a sleep over at Sue's.

"You know the trial starts on Monday?" Jack asked Neil and Rupert.

"Oh yes mate, we'll both be there for moral support" replied Neil.

"He's one bad piece of work from what sergeant Brookes told me....."said Jack.

"So what other mischief has he been up to?" asked Neil.

"Well by all accounts the police have been after him for quite some time....he's into supplying and dealing drugs as well as weapons.......he lost his driving licence some time ago as he was prosecuted for reckless driving and driving without insurance....and he's been stealing cars since he was about seventeen......and he's only twenty eight now......it makes you wonder doesn't it?" pondered Jack.

"It's a good job that he's been caught......not that it was good for you Jack" ventured Rupert "but my impression is that they have an awful lot against him and he will be in prison for quite some time".

"Well he's on a murder charge, so he'll be going away for a long time I would suspect " said Neil.

"Yes, you might be right Neil." said Jack quietly. "Anyway, I'm really glad you two can be there to support Delia and I....it means a lot."

The three men were quiet for a moment until Neil said..." stop this maudlin...come on, what do you want to drink...it's a while since we had a 'boys' night...I can't imagine the state of the house when we get back with all the girls 'pampering'!

The three men all laughed at the thought as Neil went to the bar.

*****

Just as Neil was getting the drinks in at the pub, Sue opened a bottle of prosecco for her and Delia and some nice fizzy elderflower juice for Val.

"Ok...who's going first" asked Sue "this is a really lovely face mask....it's got lavender in it and just feels gorgeous."

"I don't mind going first" said Val "I love the smell of lavender....it's so relaxing."

"I'll do you first Val, and then if I do Delia, you can do me. How does that sound?" asked Sue.

"That sounds perfect" said Delia.

As Sue got the face mask ready for Val, Delia said "It's ages since we did anything like this and I can't remember the last time I had a bit of a facial. That lavender just smells divine."

"I've got some for the feet as well but I'll have to get some towels first and a bowl with warm water.....and then I'll do your nails as well" winked Sue at Val.

"You're spoiling me" added Delia as she closed her eyes.

"And me!" joined in Val as Sue and Val looked at each other with a knowing glance.

“Well at least the children have settled which means we don’t need to worry about rushing around” said Sue.

“Has Adam gone to bed?” asked Val just as Adam came through the door.

“Not yet, auntie Val....what on earth have you got on your face” laughed Adam “you look like a ghost!”

“We’re being pampered” replied Val as best as she could without spoiling the cream on her face.

“Shouldn’t you be off to bed now, young man?” asked Sue.

“Can I just watch half an hour TV and have a drink first....pleeeeeeeze?” pleaded Adam to his mum.

“Hmm.....half an hour and no more” replied Sue who rarely could resist her adorable oldest boy. “Now shoo, whilst we have our girlie night .”

Adam laughed at his mum and her friends and went to get a drink and then into the den to watch TV for a little while.

With face masks complete, glasses topped up and their feet soaking in lavender oil warm water they all felt very relaxed.

“What’s happening about your baby shower” asked Delia. “Has your mum sorted out a date yet?”

“I spoke to her a couple of days ago” replied Sue “I think she was waiting until the trial was over so that you would feel a bit better Delia .”

“Oh she doesn’t need to do that” remonstrated Delia.

“No, it’s fine” added Val “I think we’ll all enjoy it much more once that dreadful scroat is behind bars! And anyway, there’s plenty of time yet.....”

“You hope” laughed Sue.

The three friends enjoyed their pampering session and by the time their husbands got back they had done their faces....feet, and had manicures with a lovely new nail polish that Sue had found in town, and they all felt thoroughly relaxed .

The three husbands had clearly consumed several beers as they were loud and laughing when they came in complete with bags of chips.

Delia, Sue and Val couldn't stop themselves laughing as they looked and sounded so hilarious!

"Anyone want a chip" said the three husbands together as they staggered slightly.

"I think I'll make the coffee" said Sue as the men dropped into the chairs.

When Sue came back with coffee they had eaten the chips and were definitely in need of some sobering coffee!

The girls chatted about the products they had used and how nice their skin felt whilst the men tried to be coherent, but not really succeeding, which made the three women smile at each other.

"Well I think it's about time we called for a taxi" said Val "I'm not walking home with you in this state! She said to Rupert.

"Wash stchate would that be my love?" asked Rupert staggering!

"Your drunken state" Val replied laughing.

"Well if it's ok with you Val, can we share" asked Delia "you could drop us off on the way, if you don't mind?"

"That's a good idea....I'll ring now as we may have to wait a little while" replied Val.

Val rang for the taxi which would be about twenty minutes.

"I think it will take us twenty minutes to get these two on their feet" said Val as she tried to get Rupert up who put his arms round his wife saying “do you know...you are jush gorjush....and I fink you'll make a gorjush mum......”

The three women couldn't stop laughing as this was so unlike Rupert.

“Well just get to your feet.....you drunken lout” laughed Val “the taxi will be here in a minute .“

“Taxshi.....did someone say taxshi” asked Jack who got out of his chair bolt upright.

“Yes Jack....the taxi will be here in a minute” replied Delia.

“Right mate”said Neil getting up out of the chair and shaking hands with Rupert. “I’ll shee you at the court on Monday,,,,,,don’t forget....mum’sh the word!” touching his nose.

At this Val looked at Sue with alarm in her eyes and hoped that Delia hadn’t thought anything about it whilst she sorted Jack out. Sue tried not to look alarmed and passed it off quickly saying”come on you drunken devil....the taxi just pulled up outside, so let our friends go...”

“Ok....” said Neil staggering. “Jack, my old friend....we’ll see you on Monday” as Neil pulled him into a bear hug.

Val, Delia and Sue were now laughing uncontrollably at the behaviour of their husbands. They hadn’t seen them like this for longer than they could remember and it was very funny as they could hardly stand up!

The three friends gave each other a hug and Sue told Delia to come for the children the following day when they were ready. It was Saturday so they could have a lie in, and by the look of their husbands it was doubtful they would be up before lunch. With that they all departed saying they would see each other at the court on Monday.

Chapter 42

Monday morning dawned and Sue and Neil, Delia and Jack along with Val and Rupert were all up and about early.

Everyone seemed quiet at breakfast in Sue and Neil's as they were deep in thought as to what today would bring. Sue got the children sorted out for school and without any dawdling got them on their way.

Jack's mum had arrived the day before and was happily sorting the children out ready for school, so that Delia and Jack could get themselves ready for court. Jack didn't know whether he would be called today, but the police thought it was likely, so he had to be ready. They were both nervous as it was revisiting what had happened all those weeks ago and Jack was still using a stick whilst he did physiotherapy so that his leg would heal.

Sue and Neil met Delia and Jack outside the court just before 9.30am . The trial was set for 10am but the jury would have to be sworn in first.

"I wonder where Val and Rupert are" said Delia.

"I'm sure they'll be along shortly" said Sue not daring to look at Neil. "If she's having a sicky day she'll be a bit off colour.....I'm sure she'll catch us up later."

They all went inside where Jack registered with the clerk of the court who told him that the court they needed was number six but that he would have to wait outside as he was a witness.

They found the right court and Neil, Sue and Delia all went inside after Delia gave Jack a big hug of reassurance.

The proceedings got underway quite quickly with a Judge Kenilworth presiding. The jury were sworn in no objections having been made and the prisoner was in the dock.

The prisoner, wearing a very smart suit but looking angry and truculent was asked to stand whilst the charges were read to him. The charges included far more offences than any of them knew...they included : murder, dangerous driving, driving whilst under the influence of drugs and alcohol, supplying and dealing drugs, supplying and dealing in weapons.........the list went on. Delia looked at Sue who's eyes were wide open. They couldn't believe what they had heard. When Jason Chadwick was asked how he pleaded he said "not guilty".

And so the trial began.

The prosecuting barrister brought oceans of evidence ....several police officers were asked to give evidence which they did so clearly and without stumbling, despite the defence lawyer trying hard to tie them in knots. It was clear early on that the police had been watching Jason Chadwick for some time but never been quite able to pin him down until two things happened : someone saw him shoot Jim Platt whilst trying to rob him and had video evidence of proof.

Then the dangerous driving charge when he was caught after the head-on collision with Jack's car. For the police this was the lucky breakthrough they needed as despite the evidence of the shooting he seemed to have disappeared. The police had several people in custody on related charges as he had his 'gang' who did the dirty work for him. But the police knew that Jason Chadwick was the ringleader and was responsible for so many of the crimes.

The prosecution were going through their witnesses at a fair rate of knots and no matter how hard the defence tried, they really had no defence.

The morning went swiftly by and the Judge soon called for a recess for lunch.

Delia, Sue and Neil met Jack outside but Val and Rupert still hadn't arrived and Delia was worried.

“I can’t understand why they haven’t arrived” said Delia “has she texted you Sue?”

“Oh, don’t worry. She’s perhaps a bit under the weather and Rupert may have had to work “replied Sue unconvincingly as she looked at Neil with alarm in her eyes.

“Come on” said Neil “let’s go and get a bite to eat.”

“I’m not sure I can” said Jack, clearly nervous of the proceedings.

“You need to eat Jack.....and I’m sure it won’t be as bad as you think when you get in there” added Neil “the police have got so much evidence....I think he’ll be going away for a long time!”

As they went outside the court and headed towards a little cafe that did lunches Delia stopped.....”I’m sure that’s Rupert’s car over there” she pointed.

Quick as a flash Neil said “There’s loads of cars like Rupert’s...come on I’m feeling hungry after all that procrastinating that we’ve heard this morning.”

“Oh look, there’s a table....come on before someone beats us to it .” said Sue and ushered Delia into the cafe at lightning speed.

They tried not to talk about the trial whilst they had lunch but they inevitably kept going back to it. Delia was particularly quiet during lunch and was getting quite worried.

“Are you ok?” asked Sue.

“I’m sure that’s Rupert’s car that I saw” Delia responded. “It’s just strange that we’ve not heard from either of them”.

Delia was clearly puzzled and a little upset that Val and Rupert hadn’t arrived at the court after they said they would be there.

"I think it's time to get back" said Jack .

As they were approaching the court they saw Brian outside and Sue waived.

"How's it going?" asked Brian as they approached.

"Well he's clearly got a lot of offences against him" said Jack. "Anyway, it's nice of you to turn up Brian....I didn't expect to see you here" continued Jack as he shook Brian's hand.

"All Ok?" Sue asked Brian as he nodded thoughtfully.

I don't suppose you've seen Val or Rupert have you Brian, only they said they would be here and I'm sure I saw Rupert's car, but we've not seen anything of them......" tailed off Delia.

"Yes, actually I have" replied Brian brightly "I think they've gone into the court...are you going back in .....I'll come with you if that's ok?"

As they all replied that of course it was ok the group moved into the court house ready for the afternoon's session.

As they got to court number six Rupert was waiting for them.

"Sorry, sorry for being late....you know Val...sicky icky!" laughed Rupert a little bit more forced than usual.

"Where is she?" asked Delia.

"Oh just at the ladies" replied Rupert.

"I'll go and see if she's ok" said Delia.

"No, no...." said Sue "they're calling us into court. I'll go and check on her in a few minutes if she's not back....come on, we need to go in" Sue continued ushering Delia into the court.

The group, including Brian, but not Jack who had to wait to be called, took their seats in the court moments before Judge Kenilworth arrived back to continue.

Jason Chadwick was back in the dock as several more witnesses were called . Many confirming that they had bought drugs or firearms off him. Several of them were under arrest and in custody themselves but were promised a 'lighter' sentence if they co-operated.

The prosecution lawyer then asked to call Jack Harris to the stand. Delia looked frozen on the spot and Sue took hold of her hand.

Jack came into court and took the oath. He was asked about the car crash and about the dash cam. He answered all the questions asked of him clearly and concisely .The film was shown to the court and the jury could see quite clearly that Jason Chadwick was driving at eighty miles an hour and was clearly out of control when he hit Jack's car several weeks earlier.

It was difficult for Delia and their friends to watch this piece of film as they saw clearly that Jack was lucky to be alive. Had he been in a smaller car it was unlikely that he would be here to testify. Delia was crying silently and Brian took hold of her other hand.

The defence lawyer tried hard to 'pull apart' the evidence which so clearly spoke for itself. He was on a hiding to nothing!

The Judge did ask Jack how he was recovering and thanked him for his evidence.

It was clear at this point that the Judge was getting ready to call recess for the day but the prosecution barrister jumped in very quickly just as Val quietly joined them in their seats.

"Before we consider recessing for the day, your honour, I would like to call one more witness who is crucial to the charge of murder and because of her circumstances would prefer not to delay" announced the prosecution barrister.

The defence lawyer objected saying that it was getting late in the day to hear more evidence.

The Judge called both lawyers to the bench and asked quietly what these circumstances were. The prosecution lawyer explained quietly to the judge and defence lawyer why it would be appreciated if he could call the witness.

The defence lawyer acquiesced and the Judge agreed to continue.

The prosecution lawyer asked for Mrs Alice Barton to be called to the stand.

Delia looked at Brian and then at Sue as a very heavily pregnant 'missing' Alice came into court.

Chapter 43

Alice gave her name clearly. The Judge asked her if she would like to sit as she was clearly heavily pregnant. Alice was happy to stand and so the questioning began.

For approximately twenty five minutes the prosecuting council asked her a number of questions and then asked to show the footage from a film taken on Alice's camera on the day of the shooting.

"Can you confirm that this is from your mobile phone?" asked the prosecuting council as the film started to play on a screen.

"Yes" replied Alice "that is the footage that I took".

"Whereabouts were you when you filmed it" she was asked.

"There's a corridor with a large window on the way to the ladies cloakroom where I work . I was returning from the cloakroom and stopped to look across at the rainbow that was across the sky. I took my phone out to video it.....it was very pretty" said Alice.

"Please continue" asked the barrister.

"As I was filming I saw Jim Platt walking along" she added.

"How do you know Jim Platt?" asked the barrister.

"I see him quite regularly in 'Molly's'......the little coffee shop I go in from time to time. He's often in there when I go in and one day there wasn't a table and he let me sit with him......we got on well and used to chat together ...... He was a lovely gentleman" she added quietly.

"So, can you tell me what happened next?" asked the barrister.

"As I was filming the rainbow I saw Jim walking along from the main town square.......I was about to knock on the window when I saw Jason Chadwick run up to him and push him over......Before I knew it he had shot him and was going through his pockets.......that's what I continued to film on my phone" said Alice who looked to where Brian was sat and who nodded and smiled at her.

"Mrs. Barton, did you see what happened to the gun?"

"Yes I did. He threw it down on the floor" replied Alice.

"And what happened next?"

"Well, as Jason Chadwick was taking Jim's wallet another boy ....a teenager ran up and shouted something......I couldn't quite make out what it was, but he went to Jim and tried to stop the bleeding, but within a couple of minutes people were running up and shouting for an ambulance.......a passer by grabbed the boy and kept hold of him while Jason Chadwick ran away" answered Alice.

"Did you recognise either of the people involved?" asked the barrister.

"Well yes, I did" answered Alice.

"Can you explain which you recognised and how you knew them?"

"Jason Chadwick lived near my parents over on the Sudbury housing estate when they lived there a few years ago – they've moved since, but we used to see Jason and his pals causing mischief when they were young."

What do you mean by 'mischief', Mrs. Barton?" asked the barrister.

"They used to damage cars.....break windows....steal from people......that sort of thing" said Alice.

"OBJECTION" said the defence barrister "this is just hearsay!"

"Overruled" said the Judge "I want to hear how Mrs. Barton recognised the defendant.

“Please go on Mrs. Barton” said the Judge.

“Well, one evening when I lived at home, before I was married, I watched Jason Chadwick and some of his friends take a key and scratch the length of my dad’s car....then they went jumping on the roofs of several others and damaging them......it started to make my parents ill and that’s when they moved. It seemed that the police could never quite catch them......there was never enough evidence” added Alice.

“And what about the other young man?” asked the barrister.

“Well I did recognise him as he’s been helping after school at the meet and greet centre in the cathedral. I go in sometimes when Brian, my husband, has been helping there.........his name is Martin Young and I doubt there is a bad bone in his body!” said Alice firmly.

“I would like to show the court the video film from Mrs. Barton’s mobile phone which will make her statement very clear” said the prosecuting barrister .

While the monitors were being set up the Judge asked for a chair in the witness stand so that Alice could sit down.

After a couple of minutes the footage from Alice’s phone was loaded. It started with a very clear view of a rainbow in the distance. As the film continued Jim Platt came into view and Alice clearly moved nearer to the window and as she did so Jason Chadwick came into view and showed clearly the assault and the shooting of Jim Platt, Chadwick running off having dropped the gun and then Martin Young shouting at him and going to Jim’s aid with other people then surrounding him. The picture then became blurry as Alice had moved away from the window, stopped recording, so that she could phone the police and ambulance.

As the monitors stopped there was a deathly silence in the courtroom as it was crystal clear exactly what had happened that day.

Before anyone else could speak the Judge called a recess for the following morning at 10am telling Chadwick that he might want to reconsider his verdict of not guilty!

Chapter 44

As the Judge left the courtroom Brian was out like a shot to go to Alice who was looking very peaky by the end of her evidence telling Sue that he would meet them outside.

Delia looked from Sue to Val.

"You knew didn't you......that Alice was here?"

"Not here" said Val quietly "It's complicated , but we'll explain later".

Quietly Sue, Neil, Rupert and Val followed Delia as she led the way out of the courtroom to find Jack who was waiting for them along with Brian and Alice.

"Well I have to say that this is a turn up for the books" said Jack as he shook Brian's hand. "So I take it that you were the mystery person with the evidence?" he said looking at Alice.

"It's a long story....and Delia, we didn't intentionally not tell you, but with Jack giving evidence we didn't want to put him in any danger. I promise I will tell you the full story.....but all I want to do right now is go home with Brian and sleep in my own bed" added Alice.

Delia smiled at this young woman who had caused such curiosity in the village and looked at Brian whose relief was clear to all that he had his wife back.

"I think we all need to get home" said Rupert....."you two mummies to be look absolutely bushed so let's make our way home and we'll arrange a catch up in the next few days?"

The four couples agreed that it had been a very stressful day and they needed to get home and have an early night.

After lots of hugs and handshakes they all made their way out of the court house and to the car park.

Chapter 45

The following day Delia, Sue, Rupert and Neil were all in the courtroom to hear the rest of the trial. Val was exhausted following yesterday's evidence and also supporting Alice, so they all insisted that she stayed in bed. There was no need for Brian and Alice to be there so they were surprised when Brian showed up saying that he wanted to hear the outcome and that Alice's mum was with her.

They all went for a bite to eat when the court recessed for lunch.

They took their places in the public gallery, this time along with Jack and several of the police investigation team.

When the Judge took his place and all were seated the defence barrister asked if he could speak to the Judge.

The Judge called both barristers to his bench and listened to what the defence lawyer had to say.

As the lawyers took their seats the Judge spoke to Jason Chadwick.......

"Mr Chadwick, please stand. It is my understanding that you wish to change your plea. Is this correct?"

"Yes, your honour" replied Chadwick quietly and with his head down.

The Judge asked the usher to read out the charges once more.....it was a long list of very serious offences.

"What do you now plead to the charges set before you?" asked the Judge.

"Guilty" said Chadwick quietly.

There was a gasp from people in the public gallery then the courtroom went still.

“You have pleaded guilty to some of the most serious offences imaginable and will be going to prison for a very long time” the Judge told Chadwick.

“You will be sentenced in three months time when the full impact of your crimes can be assessed. Take him to the cells” added the Judge.

As Chadwick was led away the Judge dismissed the jury thanking them for their time and also the police investigation team whose diligent work had brought this abhorrent human being to justice.

“I would, however,” said the Judge “like to pay particular tribute to Mrs Alice Barton for her extreme bravery in coming forward with such damning evidence and then taking extraordinary measures to stay safe. I know she isn’t here today but I see her husband in the public gallery and would like you to give her the gratitude of the court and wish her well when her baby is due”.

With that the Judge was up like a shot along with everyone in the court room and the trial had ended.

Jack ,Delia, Rupert, Sue and Neil all looked at one another and then at Brian who looked as bewildered as them. The police team came over along with Sergeant Brookes .

“What just happened?” Sue asked the police team.

“This does happen sometimes...... A change of plea and it can be done and dusted in no time” said one of the Inspectors on the case who then spoke directly to Brian.

“You have one very brave lady as your wife....to do what she did so that we could nail that nasty little scroat ......we take our hats off to her! Please give her our thanks when you get home and tell her to keep well.....Oh yes....we want to know what she has when the baby arrives”.

At this they all laughed and it broke the tension as they all moved to leave the courtroom.

Chapter 46

As they gathered outside the court house Sue noticed that Delia was very quiet.

“You ok, Delia?” asked Sue quietly.

“Yes, fine” was Delia’s reply.

Sue wasn’t convinced by her reply but decided not to comment at the moment.

There were hugs all round as Brian thanked them all for their support but wanted to get back to Alice to tell her what had occurred to finish the trial.

“Well who’s up for a drink?” asked Neil.

“No thanks” said Rupert “I want to go and see how Val is....she was really exhausted yesterday. But I’ll get her to call you all later.”

With that Rupert made his way over to the car park.

“Well...what about you two?“ asked Neil.

As Jack was about to agree to a drink Delia jumped in and said “No, I think we should get home then we’re there when the children come out of school.”

“Well ok then” said Neil “we’ll catch up with you soon”.

With that Delia and Jack also made their way to collect their car.

“Come on Sue....we’ll go and have a drink before we go home. We’ve still got time before the children come out of school” stated Neil.

“Ok then” agreed Sue feeling a little bit puzzled by Delia’s apparent coolness towards her.

Once comfortable in a little Bistro nearby with drinks before them Sue looked at Neil and said “Do you think Delia was a little bit off with me just then?”

“I did think it was a bit odd that they didn’t come for a drink.....Jack certainly looked as if he wanted to” replied Neil. “Why? What’s bothering you” he added.

“I can’t quite put my finger on it” Sue replied “but she definitely seemed put out with me .”

“I’ll call her when I get home and see if she’s ok” added Sue.

***

Sue missed Delia when she went to collect the children as Jack’s mother was waiting at the gate.

“Hello Betty” Sue greeted her.

“Oh hello Sue. That was a turn up for the book wasn’t it at the court....Jack didn’t expect that fellow to change his plea.” was Betty’s reply.

“No” replied Sue “It was a shock to us all. Is Delia alright....she was very quiet when we came out of court?”

I must say that she’s been very quiet since they came back....but I think she’s Ok” replied Betty “Is something the matter?”

“I’m not sure Betty to be honest....it’s just that she seemed reluctant to speak to me when we came out” said Sue “it’s probably nothing.....I’ll speak to her later.”

The children were coming out of classes so the two women exchanged cheerios and went on their way.

Sue was still deep in thought over an hour later whilst preparing the evening meal.

“A penny for them” asked Neil.

“Hmm” replied Sue.

“A penny for them......what’s on your mind...you’re certainly not here!” came Neil’s reply.

Sue put down the pan she was cooking with and looked at Neil.

"I don't know....but I think something was bothering Delia and it was to do with me....but I can't figure out what!" exclaimed Sue clearly upset.

"In which case I suggest you give her a call after tea" said Neil taking hold of Sue and giving her a hug. "It's probably nothing, so don't let it upset you...now come on...let's get food on the table. I'm starving!" At which Sue laughed and called the children to their meal.

After tea Neil got the children into the bath and told Sue to ring Delia. Before she did she called Val.

"Hi Val" said Sue as Val answered the phone "how are you feeling?"

"Hi Sue. I'm fine thanks. Definitely better for having a rest today. Hasn't it been a stressful week? I'm glad the scroat decided to plead guilty....it made it easy for the jury " came Val's reply. "Anyway...are you OK?"

"Well I'm ok, but Delia was a bit off with me earlier and I wondered if you could think of something that I've done for her to be cool with me?" replied Sue.

"Delia. Off with you?No, I can't think of any reason...that's strange. Are you sure you're not imagining it?" said Val.

"I don't think so. We've known each other long enough to recognise the signs. I'm going to ring her and ask her" said Sue firmly.

"Well let me know if there is something wrong" replied Val.

"Ok. I'll speak to you later" said Sue.

Sue immediately phoned Delia's number and Jack answered.

"Hi Jack. It's Sue. Is Delia there?"

"Ermm...no she's a bit tied up at the moment" came Jack's reply.

"Oh" said Sue "can you ask her to ring me when she's finished what she's doing?"

"Yes. I'll pass the message on" came Jack's reply and with that Jack hung up

leaving Sue with the phone still in her hand and feeling very puzzled.

Sue immediately phone Val back and told her what had transpired and also told Val that she was feeling most uncomfortable about the way Jack had been with her.

"What should I do Val?" asked Sue "We've never fallen out and always been able to talk to each other" Sue was now on the verge of tears.

"I'll tell you what...." said Val "give me half an hour then come and collect me and we'll go round and see if she is ok . Neil will be ok with the children for an hour or so and Delia will have theirs in bed by the time we get there so she can't refuse to see us."

Sue thought for a moment.

"Are you still there?" asked Val.

"Yes. I'm just thinking. What if she refuses? What then?" asked Sue.

"Sue. She will not refuse when we turn up! Get yourself sorted and come and collect me. I'll see you in half an hour" instructed Val.

"Ok. I'll see you shortly" said Sue.

Once Sue had explained to Neil that she and Val were going to see Delia and find out what was going on she got herself ready and drove to Val's who was ready and waiting for her. It only took them ten minutes to reach Delia's and they knocked on the door for it to be opened by Jack who just looked at them for a moment.

"You had better come in" said Jack reluctantly "Delia is in the kitchen."

Val and Sue went straight in to where Delia was sitting obviously having been crying.

"What on earth....." said Sue putting her arms round Delia who immediately burst into tears .

"What's going on Delia?" asked Val.

Delia was sobbing and it took her some time to calm down by which time Val had put the kettle on and got mugs out of the cupboard. Once the tea was made Delia had calmed down and Jack had left the three women together, realising that he wasn't welcome!

"You knew...both of you. All this time you knew and never told me!" said Delia getting upset again.

Sue and Val looked at each other clearly puzzled.

"We knew what?" asked Val.

"You knew all about Alice being hidden and pregnant and didn't tell me" replied Delia clearly upset.

"Oh. My. Goodness!" said Sue quietly. "It's not like that at all Delia...honestly. We still don't know the full story. But you did know that Val had seen her at the ante-natal clinic. I only know some of what happened because I challenged Brian after Val's mum had seen Dennis the demon in Spain and Brian asked for our help. What we couldn't do was compromise Jack's evidence because of knowing about Alice."

"In keeping quiet what little we did know we were protecting you and Jack until everything was finished" added Val going to Delia and giving her a hug.

"It will all become clear soon. Alice has promised to tell us exactly what happened.... I think she just needs some time at home with Brian" said Sue "she has been under a lot of strain......as has Brian because of all the secrecy in keeping her hidden. Especially with the gossiping that went on at first."

"Now....does that put things right?" demanded Val smiling.

Delia looked first at Sue and then at Val and nodded slowly.

"When I saw Alice in the court and you both clearly knowing that she was a witness.....I felt completely at a loss as to why you hadn't included me.......I can see why you couldn't....I'm just a bit bruised at the moment" said Delia a bit tearily.

"You must be glad that it's all over now though?" asked Val.

"Absolutely" said Delia breathing a deep sigh of relief. "I never want to go through those weeks after the accident ever again.......seeing Jack the way he was........" Delia tailed off.

The three friends talked and laughed together for some time before Val started to yawn.

"Come on you" said Sue "it's time all yummy mummies were in bed! I'll take you home."

The three women exchanged hugs and agreed that they would all be in church on Sunday as they were curious to see the faces of some of the gossips when they saw Alice in church and to be there to give both Alice and Brian any support they needed.

Chapter 47

Sunshine greeted Sunday morning and Sue wondered how many would be in church as word had got round that a heavily pregnant Alice was home. She hadn't yet been named in the press as being a main witness in one of the biggest trials that Willington had seen in a long time. Brian particularly hoped that it would stay that way especially as he had received a call from the prison where Jason Chadwick had been taken, asking if he would pay Chadwick a visit. So far Brian hadn't decided as he couldn't work out why Chadwick would want to see him.

Sue got to church a little earlier so that she was there when Alice arrived. Val and Rupert also arrived early as Val wanted to be there for support as her and Alice had become good friends since being at ante-natal appointments at similar times.

As soon as Alice saw Val she gave her a hug along with Sue, and she went to sit with Rupert and Val.

Sue went into the vestry to speak to Brian who looked about ten years younger now that Alice was back.

"Good morning daddy to be" exclaimed Sue to Brian who beamed from ear to ear.

"Sue...I'll never be able to thank you enough for your help and support over these last few weeks and months.........I'm just so glad it's all over and Alice is back home with me.......the relief is huge!" said Brian.

"No problem Brian......we are all so delighted that Alice is here...and the baby...well it goes without saying that we are delighted" replied Sue. "Anyway, we better get this show on the road....the pews are filling up nicely."

"Do you think people are being nosy Sue, knowing that Alice is back?" asked Brian.

“Brian....there are always going to be the nosy parkers no matter what happens....just let’s hope they fill the collection plates” said Sue laughing as she left Brian to ‘gown up’.

It was clear that whilst some people were curious to see that Alice really was back, many were concerned that they had missed her and wanted to know when the baby was due and the usual questions.

Whilst Sue was clearing things away after the service, she heard the quiet parp, parp, parp and smiling to herself knew that farting Freddie was approaching.....poor old Freddie she thought to herself!

“Hello there young Sue” said Freddie’s familiar voice as Sue looked up.

“Hello Freddie. How are you today?” Sue asked.

“I’m champion” replied Freddie “ and I am DELIGHTED to see that our Alice is here amongst us again....and having a baby”.

“Yes. It is good news Freddie” agreed Sue.

Do you know where she has been all this time?” asked Freddie.

“No Freddie. Not really. I’m sure that Alice will tell us when she is ready – if she is able to tell us where she has been. You do know that she was a crucial witness in the Chadwick trial last week?” added Sue.

“Ah. Now that explains a lot. I had heard something like that but I wasn’t really sure and I didn’t want to distress Brian by asking.” said Freddie just as Alice walked up behind them.

“Freddie. Aren’t I going to get a hug?” asked Alice.

Freddie turned with a huge smile and gave Alice a hug that nearly squashed her.

"My dear, dear girl....you have no idea how delighted I am to see you...and looking so well......radiant in fact!"

"Well I'm home now and won't be going anywhere again in a hurry. Just don't believe everything you hear Freddie. In time it will become clear but for now I just want to be home with Brian and get the nursery ready" said Alice smiling at them both.

"Come on....let's go and get a coffee amongst the throngs!" laughed Alice.

At this the three walked down to the meeting room where refreshments were being served . There were lots of greetings to Alice from the parishioners who were clearly very delighted to see her. Both Sue and Alice observed Brenda making a get away when Alice came into the room. The two women smiled at each other knowing full well that Brenda would just make more gossip given the opportunity!

As people drifted off Val and Rupert came to say cheerio to Alice along with Delia and Jack. Alice said to them all "Are you doing anything on Friday evening?"

"I don't think so" said Delia "Why?"

"I would like to invite you all, as well as Sue and Neil to a little buffet supper" said Alice "nothing fancy.....but I'd like to say thank you to you all properly."

"You don't need to do that" said Neil joining the conversation.

"I really would like you all to come" said Alice "and so would I" added Brian as he joined the group.

"I'm sure my mum will babysit" said Neil.

"And my mum's not going home, just yet" added Jack.

"And we don't have that problem....... yet!" laughed Rupert.

"Well it's a date then" said Alice "about 7.30 ok?"

The time was agreed and the friends said their farewells as Sue ushered them out of church so that she could lock up and go home to start the Sunday dinner!

Chapter 48

Friday evening arrived and Val & Rupert picked Delia and Jack up and Sue and Neil walked to the vicarage all arriving together just before 7.30pm.

Brian greeted them all with glasses of fizz which the friends gladly took except for Val and Alice who weren't drinking whilst pregnant.

Alice had laid out a beautiful buffet for them in the dining room and once coats were taken and drinks re-filled they all ooohed and awed about the feast!

The four couples sat and enjoyed the wonderful buffet that Alice had put together. The men talked a lot about football whilst there was lots of baby talk amongst the ladies. Alice showed the 'girls' the nursery that Brian had been painting . Alice had chosen lemon with little elephants on a border.

"I decided on a neutral colour as we don't know what we're having.....we want it to be a surprise!" Alice told them. "What about you Val....do you know what you're having?"

"No. Like you Alice, we decided to wait until it's born......I know that Rupert is a bit impatient , but I wanted the surprise as well. So we've started thinking in tones of cream. We can always add some colour once the baby is here" replied Val.

"Well I think it's absolutely gorgeous" said Sue smiling and Delia nodded in agreement.

They rejoined the men and they all went to sit in the lounge whilst Brian went off to make coffee which he brought in and handed to everyone.

Alice cleared her throat and said "I'm going to tell you all what happened".

"You don't need to do that Alice, we are all just thankful that you are safe and back with us" stated Sue.

"Well thanks for that Sue, but I really do want you to know as you've been such a wonderful support, not just to me but to Brian as well." Alice responded.

"We both feel that we want you to know what really happened" added Brian.

"So....here goes" said Alice.

"It started with the shooting of poor Jim Platt. That afternoon when it all happened I had just been to the cloakroom at work to get my things as I was about to meet Brian. There's a bay type window that runs part way along the corridor and I paused for a moment to look out and saw a rainbow.......the thing is I've had two miscarriages over the past couple of years and when I saw the rainbow I felt it was a sign that everything would be ok. I was meeting Brian to go for the scan and it just seemed right.....do you know what I mean?"

I know exactly what you mean......a 'rainbow' baby...." commented Sue.

"Yes just that" added Alice.

"I don't know what you mean" said Rupert.

"Well....if you've had a miscarriage and then had a baby, they call that baby a 'rainbow baby'" said Alice.

"Oh.....I'm with you.....so you're thinking was seeing the rainbow was a sign "said Neil.

"Yes" said Alice "so I switched my phone to camera and started videoing it – it really was beautiful. Anyway, while I'm doing this Chadwick attacked and shot poor Jim Platt....you see I got to know Jim when I went in 'Molly's'.....it's where Brian took me the first time we met" added Alice as Brian looked across at her with a smile so full of love Sue filled up .

"Well obviously at that point I carried on filming....the young boy that ran up was nothing to do with Chadwick but someone saw him take the gun when Chadwick dropped it. While I was still filming Chadwick looked up and I thought he had seen me – even though I moved out of the way quickly, I was aware that he may have recognised me.....I certainly recognised him! I really was in a bit of a fluster and actually very frightened.....if he had seen me, or recognised me then I knew that I was in danger. I quickly rang Brian and told him what had happened and he met me at the office and we went home."

At this point Brian took over." I have a friend in the police so I rang him. He came round and looked at the video footage that Alice had taken and was delighted that the evidence would put Chadwick away for a long time.....but it had also put Alice in danger and we really, really did not want to lose this baby" Brian said as Alice took hold of his hand.

Alice picked up the story...." the police immediately wanted me to go into some sort of a protected house....but I really did not want to do that. So after discussion with the police, the Bishop and of course Dennis, we came up with a plan. Brian has an aunt living in Buryfield in a house with plenty of space. She is totally discreet. She agreed to hide me there, but also look after me, bless her. Brian was so worried about the impact on me and he needed to be able to visit without too much suspicion and as he visits her regularly it was fine."

Alice paused for a moment.

"This is where it gets a bit devious, and I really hope you won't judge us too badly and, most of all, you will keep this part to yourselves."

The group were listening carefully and all nodded in agreement that whatever Alice and Brian told them wouldn't leave the four walls.

"Brenda...." said Alice as everyone groaned and Alice laughed "is rather a gossip".

"Don't we know it!" said Delia.

"But she came in rather useful for our plan" said Alice.

"We knew when she came to do the flowers, and that she comes on her bike and we can see her coming up the lane from our back bedroom window......so we came up with a plan ."

Brian took up the story...."Dennis...the Archdeacon had been struggling for a while with who he actually is".

"What do you mean 'who he is'" asked Neil.

"He's gay Neil...and he's been struggling to come to terms with it and with his position. But a while ago he met Gordon when he went on holiday and he knew that he had to make a decision as he wanted to be with Gordon. He had discussed it with the Bishop who had given him time to think it through. Dennis had come to the decision to move to Spain and make a life with Gordon and had only told me a few days earlier that he was getting ready to leave" said Brian.

"Dennis and Brian have been friends since college days so it was natural that he would tell Brian first" said Alice taking up the story again.

"Anyway, we arranged that I would be seen to 'go away' with Dennis at the exact time that Brenda was coming on her bike to do the flowers. I put a few things in the biggest suitcase that we have so it looked as if I was going for good and Dennis could haul it into his car......Brian was acting as 'look out' in the bedroom while Dennis was behind the front door and I was with him. The minute Brian saw her coming down the lane we had to time it precisely." Alice stopped for breath but then continued "honestly, if it hadn't been such a serious situation we would all have been falling about laughing.......Brenda's face was a picture when she saw Dennis dragging the suitcase with me following behind! It was no wonder she fell off her bike " said Alice.

By this time Sue couldn't contain herself with laughter and one by one they all joined in. Brian went to make some more drinks whilst the hilarity of them discussing Brenda falling off her bike continued. Once their drinks were refreshed Alice took up the story........" we had to make it look as convincing as possible" she said seriously. "We all knew that if the Chadwick gang found out who had seen the shooting and where I was that I wouldn't be here for long.

Brian's aunt is an absolute gem. She bought me that little brunette wig, got me clothes that I wouldn't normally wear....though I was starting to need maternity clothes.....and generally made me comfortable and looked after. The big problem was that I couldn't tell my mum and dad as it put would them at serious risk.......I know they were very worried and couldn't understand why I had 'left' Brian....they know the full story now however ......much to their relief!" added Alice.

"We let Brenda do her worst around the village" said Brian "knowing that Sue wouldn't let her get away with it in a hurry......."

"No! I certainly didn't!" said Sue as everyone laughed.

"I went to see Alice every week on my day off and some evenings when I could get away....and obviously the ante-natal appointments. Now that was when we got worried" as he looked over at Val "as we saw Val there, and I was fairly certain Val had seen me"....

"Oh yes! I had....but thought I was mistaken until Delia's Mum saw Dennis in Spain and I saw Alice wearing a brunette wig!" said Val.

"Oh, we didn't know about that until Sue came and confronted me" laughed Brian. Then of course, Jack had the accident and Chadwick was caught. The police had been going round in circles trying to capture him....he was very elusive. I'm sorry, Jack, that they had to capture him with you suffering though. The police had loads of evidence to arrest him and his drug dealing crowd, but the problem was finding them."

"What was all that about at the Easter Eggstravaganza when those lads came looking for trouble" asked Sue "Were they involved?"

"No Sue, they weren't....they were doing just that....looking for trouble, and after all the work you had put into it we weren't going to let them start spoiling things which is why Neil and I cleared them away " added Brian.

"Once we knew when the trial was the difficulty was getting me there without the press getting to know and disclosing my name" said Alice " and that's where Val and Rupert and Sue and Neil helped. I had to get close by to be ready to testify without being seen, so Val and Rupert offered to let me stay with them and then transfer to Sue's just before the trial in order to put anyone off the scent who may have been watching.......We had to keep Brian out of the way and that was the worst bit" said Alice shaking her head.

"We couldn't risk involving you and Jack" Alice told Delia "as we didn't want Jack to be aware of any of the video so that he wouldn't be able to comment......I just hope you don't think too badly of us for not sharing, but we wanted to keep you safe as well" added Alice.

"I was a little hurt when I realised that something had been going on...but I'm ok. I realise how serious it was and that you had to be protected...and I'm just glad that Jack's evidence helped to put him away" said Delia.

"The police have convinced us that we are safe....the whole gang has been rounded up and they will be away for a very long time" commented Brian "the interesting thing is that Chadwick asked to see me last week and I really couldn't figure out why. After a lot of thought I decided to visit him. He thanked me for seeing him and asked me to apologise for the distress he has caused."

"No! You are kidding" said Sue.

"No. Straight up. He said that he recognised Alice when she testified and he remembered all the things he'd done as a kid and felt ashamed. That's why he changed his plea. He said that he knows he's done a lot of bad things and will try very hard to amend his ways in prison." Brian concluded.

"That is a turn up for the book" said Jack as surprised as the others.

"Well now you have the full story and hopefully we can all enjoy the summer holidays.....Alice and I are off to see Dennis in Spain" Brian told them.

At which the group all discussed their holiday plans for the next hour or so before it was clear that Alice and Val were tired and needed their sleep so the group said their thanks for a lovely evening and went home to their beds.

Chapter 49

The following Thursday Val, Sue and Delia all met in their favourite place 'Mugs with Hugs' and ordered their usual hot chocolate and coffees and cookies. Just after they had ordered Alice came in and was warmly greeted by them all.

"Come and sit with us" said Delia.

"I don't want to interrupt" replied Alice.

"Come on, you daft thing....you're more than welcome" said Val. " Have you just been to ante-natal?"

"Yes I have" replied Alice "I just needed something sweet to lift my energy" she added as Kathy brought Alice a hot chocolate across.

Just as the four women were swopping notes about ante-natal care the door opened and in waltzed Brenda with one of her friends .

"Well I knew , of course that she was pregnant....you could tell in her face...." said Brenda and stopped abruptly as she saw Alice, Val, Sue and Delia all look up at her.

Brenda quickly retreated out of the shop as the four women laughed at the look on her face when she spotted them.

"I don't think she'll try to come in here again" said Kathy from behind the counter.

The summer holidays arrived for the children at the end of the following week with Adam leaving to go to 'big' school in September and holiday plans for the break having been made.

Delia and Jack were travelling north to see his mum and sister and then going over to Ireland for a couple of weeks.

Sue, Neil and the children were going to the Canaries for the sun and sand .....not to mention the Sangria according to Neil.

Val and Rupert were going to Lake Garda in Italy deciding that once the baby arrives their holiday plans will be very different.

The holidays flew by. Adam started High school. Maisie and Flora and Bobby and Joe all moved into new classes when they returned to school and Val and Alice both looked huge with babies!

As a beautiful September developed into a golden autumn the excitement over the forthcoming births were highlighted when Sue and Delia organised baby showers for both Val and Alice. They managed to arrange them without either women finding out and they were delighted with the generous gifts that people had brought.

Sue had just returned from taking the children to school when the phone rang. It was Val.

"Sue" said Val rather breathless as Sue answered the phone. "Sue....aaaahh"

"Oh dear...I know that sound" answered Sue "Have you phoned Rupert?"

"Yeeeees!" said Val " but he's stuck in traffic and told me to ring you".

"Ok Val . I'll be with you in a few minutes" replied Sue.

It was obvious to Sue that Val was in labour and she needed someone with her until Rupert got home. She gathered her belongings...left Neil a note in case she was out when he came home at lunch time, and drove to Val's.

Val had opened the front door ready for Sue's arrival so Sue went straight in to find her friend leaning over a chair taking deep breaths.

"When did this start Val" asked Sue very aware that Val was well into her labour.

"About..........an hour...........after Rupert left" Val said between gritted teeth.

"He's on his way" Sue told her. "I spoke to him in the car on the way......but I think we need to ring the hospital and get them ready for your arrival" said Sue who found the number amongst all the 'baby' things that Val had put together.

Sue phoned the hospital and told them that Val was in labour and that the contractions were about four minutes apart. The midwife told Sue to get Val ready to go to hospital and when they got to three minutes to take her.

For the next half hour Sue rubbed Val's back and counted the minutes in between the contractions. Half an hour later, and just as Rupert ran through the door they increased to three minutes apart.

"Right Rupert.....go now. You need to take Val straight to the hospital....her contractions are three minutes apart and the midwife said to take her" instructed Sue.

As Sue and Rupert helped Val into the car Val's waters broke.

"Oh no! Sue....what am I going to do? I'm sure the baby's coming....." exclaimed Val.

Sue ran back inside and phoned the midwife again and explained what had happened.

The midwife told Sue to get her back inside and they would send the on call midwife as it didn't look as if they had time to get her to the hospital. The midwife gave her instructions and Sue went back to the car.

"Get her back inside Rupert....they're sending a midwife here ....they don't think there is time to get her to the hospital now that her water's have gone" Sue told him.

Gently Sue and Rupert manoeuvred Val back into the house where Sue ran around getting the things together that the midwife had instructed. They got Val as comfortable as they could, Sue was acutely aware that this baby wasn't hanging around! Just at the point where Sue was telling Rupert to help Val with her breathing and realising that she was going to have to deliver this baby, the doorbell rang and the midwife had arrived.

It took seconds for the midwife to realise that the baby was about to be born and she got straight into delivery mode asking for Sue's help. The delivery kit, towels and warm water were all ready and within minutes of the midwife's arrival Val gave birth to her baby son.

The midwife handed the baby to Val whilst Rupert had tears running down his cheeks and Sue openly cried at seeing her friend's son brought into the world.

The midwife dealt with sorting out Val and gave the baby to his dad to hold who had immediately fallen in love with him.

"Do you have a name for him?" asked the midwife.

As Val looked at Rupert they both said together "James".

"Oh that's lovely" said Sue as Rupert handed the baby to her.

"He is absolutely beautiful" said Sue tearily.

Once mum and baby were clearly fine Sue said that she would go and get some

supplies for them. Having expected the baby to be born in hospital they were short of a few bits and pieces.

The midwife stayed for a little while to check that both mother and baby were ok and then left telling them that another midwife would call later in the day.

Val soon fell asleep and Rupert dotingly held his new born son for a long time before placing him in the crib so that he could make the many phone calls that were now needed. He didn't think that he had ever known his heart to be full of such love.

When Sue arrived back at Val's a couple of hours later the congratulations had already started coming in. There was the most beautiful bouquet of flowers from Rodney and Chrissy and Val's mum was on her way over along with Nina, Rupert's mum. Sue decided that once they arrived she would leave them to it as she didn't want to intrude on family time.

Lynn, Val's Mum and Nina arrived at almost the same time and were so excited.

"I understand you helped with the delivery" Nina asked Sue.

"Well I was here.....but the midwife delivered him" replied Sue.

"Don't be so modest" shouted Val who had heard the conversation.....

"she was brilliant!"

Sue decided that it was time for her to go as she would have to collect the children from school before too long and they would be very excited when she told them about the baby.

As she walked through her front door Sue saw that the answer machine light was flashing so went to check it.

"Sue, Sue is it right....has Val had the baby and you were with her?" was the message from Delia. Sue smiled at the excitement in her friend's voice so rang her back immediately and told her about the birth.

"Anyway, she seems ok....she didn't panic and the baby came quickly" Sue concluded.

Delia said that she would speak to her the following day and with her head in a whirl Sue went to collect the children from school. They were very excited and wanted to see the baby but Sue told them that they would have to wait a few days until everything had calmed down, but she agreed to take them shopping for a teddy bear the following day.

When the excitement had calmed down and the children had eaten tea Sue decided to let Alice and Brian know about Val's baby. She didn't get an answer when she phoned so left a message to ring her when they got back.

When the children were all in bed Sue went through the whole story again with Neil who was as delighted as Sue that the baby was ok and that Val was alright.

Sue felt exhausted and decided to have an early night only realising when she got in bed that neither Alice or Brian had phoned her back.

The following morning Delia dropped the children off at Sue's for her to take them to school as she had one of her days out of town and Sue had promised to take and collect them from school. Delia dropped Adam off on her way which was a big treat for him as he didn't have to get the early bus.

The children duly dropped at school Sue came home to sort out in the house and do Neil's accounts. She had only just started on the accounts when the phone rang and she knew from the caller display that it was Brian or Alice.

Sue picked up the phone and before she could speak Brian said :

"I'm so sorry I didn't get back to you last night Sue.......I was at the hospital" he said at high speed.

"The hospital?" questioned Sue. "Are you ok?"

"I'm fine...........it's Alice..." he replied.

"Oh my goodness.....is she alright?" asked Sue

"They're fine....."replied Brian.

"They....." asked Sue.

"She had the baby last night.....only it's not baby, but babies.......we've got twins.....I can't believe it Sue......twins....a boy and a girl" said a very emotional Brian.

"Well that's wonderful news Brian......have you eaten?" asked Sue.

"Eeerrrm.......not since sometime yesterday........." Brian tailed off.

"Then get yourself over here right away and I'll cook you some breakfast" Sue told him.

"Are you sure?" asked Brian.

"By the time you get here the bacon will be done and the eggs on the go....so get a move on!" Sue told him.

Sue set to immediately and within a few minutes a very dishevelled, unshaven Brian was at her door looking absolutely shell shocked.

As Brian tucked into the breakfast that Sue had prepared she told Brian that Val had also had her baby the day before and the circumstances of the delivery. It appeared that at the time Val was having her baby Alice went into labour and got to hospital.

"She was in a slow labour for what seemed like ages and then they decided to put a drip up to help things along" Brian told Sue.

"Did you know that you were having twins?" asked Sue.

"No we didn't....apparently it's very unusual today for it not to be picked up on a scan, but sometimes it happens......." tailed off Brian.

"Have you chosen names for them?" asked Sue.

"Not completely.....but we think it will be Grace for the girl and Andrew for the boy" said Brian.

"Oh how lovely" said Sue telling Brian to go and sit in the lounge and she would bring him some coffee.

When Sue went back into the lounge with coffee for Brian he was fast asleep in the chair so she tip toed out and left him to sleep closing the door quietly behind her.

A couple of hours later just after Sue had finished doing Neil's accounts and she had gone into the kitchen to make a drink the lounge door opened and a bleary eyed Brian appeared.

"Sue, why did you let me sleep?" asked Brian as the front door opened and Neil appeared.

"Because you were clearly exhausted" replied Sue.

"Hello Brian" said Neil as he walked in looking puzzled at Brian's appearance.

"Alice has had the baby.....well babies actually Neil....she's had twins!" Sue told him.

"Well congratulations Brian....what are they...boys...girls...?" asked Neil.

"One of each....a boy and a girl" replied Brian waking up.

"I think there is about twelve hours between Val having James and Alice having the twins....but the same day.....how good is that" said Sue excitedly.

"I think I'd better be going" said Brian.

"Oh come and have some lunch man before the real work starts" laughed Neil.

Sue and Neil persuaded him to stay for lunch before he went back to the hospital.

When Brian had gone Sue phoned Val to ask how she was and to tell her about Alice and the twins. Val was excited to know that they had both had their babies on the same day.

"I'm glad I didn't have surprise twins" Val told Sue.

“I know....they really will have their work cut out” agreed Sue.

Word got round the village very quickly that Alice had had twins and the generosity of people was outstanding. They received more baby clothes in pink and blue over the next few days than they could ever have imagined.

The knitters in the congregation had knit both blue and pink expecting either Val or Alice to have a boy or girl, so there was plenty of variety.

There were presents for Val and Rupert and presents for Alice and Brian from shawls to cardigans and a surprise double buggy that turned up by special delivery.

“Now I wonder who that could be from!” Brian said to Alice when it arrived.

They knew full well that it could only be from Freddie, so when he phoned later to ask how they were they just thanked him profusely before he claimed not to know what they were talking about and then laughed his indomitable laugh!

The village couldn’t have been more full of joy that early October week. Even Brenda had knitted a little cardigan which Alice accepted graciously. Flags and bunting announced the arrival of all three babies with congratulations banners in all the shops. It was a really joyous time and the new mums shared plenty of stories of sleepless nights and nappy changes over the next few weeks.

Chapter 50

The church was full to the brim on the first Sunday in advent with a clear blue sky and a crisp frost on the ground.

The two families were at the front ready for the baptisms of James Gregory Wilson and Grace Amelia and Andrew John Barton.

The Bishop of Willbury was officiating at this very special service and there was a warmth in the church that hadn't been felt for some time.

Dennis was there with Gordon as Alice and Brian had asked him to be Godfather to Andrew along with Neil and Brian's sister who was to be Godmother. Freddie was Godfather to Grace and her Godmothers were to be Sue and Brian's aunt.

Val and Rupert had asked Rodney, Delia, Sue and Jack to be James's Godparent's.

As the Bishop brought each baby to baptism there wasn't a dry eye in the church. It was a long time since twins had been baptised....and never to their own vicar, so it was indeed a very special occasion.

Val and Rupert had starting attending regularly and had been taken to the hearts of the congregation as Rupert had a wicked sense of humour and frequently teased the old dears who loved it.

During the service the advent ring was lit and towards the end of the service each baby was given a candle with their name on it, specially commissioned by Freddie.

The whole church was invited to the Christening lunch which was to take place in the Parish Hall which had been beautifully decorated in pink and blue courtesy of Rodney and Chrissy Melker.

Rupert had insisted on providing the buffet, despite Brian's protestations, but adding that he could do it next time!

When the Bishop said grace and toasted the three babies, everyone cheered.....even Brenda!

Printed in Great Britain
by Amazon